The Gods Are Mortal

Novel

Chapter Two

Igowe and Gwons will combat for supremacy. This battle is a decider on which kingdom will possess Egwolom-a goldmine in the borderline of their territories for the next hundred decades. In a sacred grove, the kingdoms' warriors gather to decide a setting for the war.

A guest chief priest from another land performs the rite of dipping a purple prediction cowry into a calabash filled with limewater for ten minutes. He washes the cowry until it turns white, cleans it with cotton, and then places the cowry on a lavender bed. Afterwards, he leaves the arena in rotating steps.

The priests from Gwons and Igowe respectively step forward. They polish the cowry with black and gold colour. A rocket lightening from the sky breaks the cowry into two-the gold and black pieces.

The priest of Gwons puts the cowries inside a dark hourglass and bows. They turn to the warrior camp of Igowe and both gestures for any warrior to come forward and pick a cowry.

Omena, the head warrior walks towards the stage but Keme stops him. Omena questioningly stares at Keme's hand on his arm. Keme slowly shakes his head, his smoky eyes softly beg for cooperation. Omena shrugs but Keme holds him firmly.

To all fantasy fiction lovers

Chapter One

Edion is a sky god. The people of Igowe believe in Edion, that he and his subordinate deities munificently rule over the affairs of humans. They always give sacrifices of praise and provisions to thank the gods for protecting them. Other deities respect him as the chief of gods; all deities call him *Lord Eternal*. All deities rise when he stands, and sits when he rises from his throne. All deities bow as he walks with a white dove perched on his left arm.

Today is another phase of judgement. Many souls assemble before Edion for him to assign a final resting or restless place for them. The goddess of fertility comes before Edion, she kneels, "My Lord, the cry of your heir has pierced the ears of the goddesses."

"This is great news. I am ecstatic; all souls will have fair hearings. This calls for a great celebration. Let the heaven crier spread the news all over the kingdom. My heir has been born, finally, I have a successor, and he shall sit at my right hand." The dove chirps excitedly. "Let all souls come forward and receive blessings."

The first soul comes forward and bows. He is happy for Edion.

"Oh, Chuko, welcome, welcome to the upper world, I hope your stay on earth was not that bad," says Edion.

"Yes, it was not. I am most grateful. My Lord Eternal, here is a little gift for the new born," Chuko offers a silver cutlass to Edion. "It was my precious farm tool. I was working very hard on my farm when I slumped and died. I had no idea of the wee one's arrival. I would have brought something more befitting for your heir. Please, accept my humble present."

Edion gestures the angel at his right hand to accept the gift. "You are a very generous soul. It will be useful to my heir, I shall call him Erin, and he shall have the qualities of thunderbolts and vengeance. Perhaps, he will someday wield this cutlass to avenge a crime. I am sure your gift will be useful. Welcome once again to the upper world."

"Thank you, my Lord Eternal; it is an honour to be in your realm."

"But look at the mirror." Chuko gazes at the golden mirror framed with dragon claws. "The people have left your clothes at your graveside. This shows they are displeased with you. You were not nice on earth. The people are not happy to share the properties of a wicked person. Chuko, was I wrong in my judgement of your character?"

"No, my Lord Eternal, the god can never be wrong. I was good, but the people spare little love for the penury stricken man. The earthlings now cherish material things more than a man's character. As you can see, my clothes are not expensive and most of them are tattered. I was a very poor farmer whose work clothes could not be distinguished from his ceremonial attire."

Edion sighs. "This means I was not fair to you. You worked so hard, yet wealth did not reward your labour. But why? I know I blessed your destiny with riches."

"You're most fair, my Lord Eternal. The gods are wise. But riches were my enemy; they never shared a cup with me. Riches never stepped onto my threshold."

"Wealth was proposed to flood your household. No, I was not fair to your lifetime. There is no afterlife for you here. You shall return to earth and be born with silver spoon. However, your wealth will attract your death. Do you agree?"

"Something must kill a man. My Lord Eternal, yes I agree. I suffered very much. Let me enjoy fame and wealth." Chuko bows and kisses Edion's feet.

"There is one more thing," Edion raises a finger. "This is your afterlife. It is the second and the last chance to live on earth. At the end of your lifetime, you will never exist. Not on earth and not in the upper world."

Chuko looks confused. He wriggles his hands and bows dejectedly, "My Lord Eternal, where will my soul go?"

"You will become a star. You shall live in the cloud."

Chuko bows happily, "I wholeheartedly agree my Lord Eternal. Lead me to the path where I would be reborn."

"Go to the goddess of fertility. She shall prepare you for the rite of silver womb. A couple has sought for a child they will name, Omena. You will be a great warrior of your time."

Chuko bows and hurries off, he is happy that his soul will receive another body. He steps into the den of rebirth. It is a very wet tube. He slips and spirals down. He lands with his buttocks. The goddess of fertility opens a small tree with warm optimal temperature. Flowery tissues clot the inner walls of the tree. She ushers him to go in.

Chuko peers into the tree. He rears away from the steam and goes to stand by the goddess. "It is filled with so many mild flowers, yet it is warm in there. How can I stay in it?"

"The flowers look fresh, correct?"

"Yes but," he points at the tree…

She claps her hands impatiently, "No but, it will not smother but keep you fresh. Now, go in."

Chuko steps onward, "The source of my birth is supposed to be a cool place. How will I survive in this heat? Besides, it is very small."

"Am I not a big god? A big god has to inject you into the tree tube. Do not worry. You would fit into it. You will become little and very fragile once you are in. Only a warm sphere will keep you safe. Go in for your cells to be reborn. You will be out in exactly nine month. If there is a delay of an hour, kick the tree with your limbs and I will come forth to deliver you." Chuko nods and happily walks in. He turns around. The goddess of fertility chants some incantations and he transforms into a foetus.

Edion summons Agbavwo, the angel that formed Chuko's destiny, "Agbavwo, you were meant to control Chuko's fate, he was never meant to be a peasant farmer. Tell me what you did, and tell me righteously." Agbavwo looks at his feet. Edion softly raps his fingers on the throne's armrest, "You cannot look me in the face because you are guilty of something."

Agbavwo quickly falls on his knees and joins his palms, "I'm sorry, my Lord Eternal. I swapped his destiny with a favourite being."

"You swapped a human's destiny? Who made you a decider of man's fate? Your only duty is to guide them to fulfil and live the life carved out for them."

Agbavwo slowly lies on the floor, "My Lord Eternal, please pardon this folly."

"It's a great folly indeed, and you shall receive punishment for it."

"My Lord Eternal, I beg your pardon. I swear on my powers that I will never commit such a folly again."

"Meaning you will carry out other misdemeanours?"

"My Lord Eternal, you misconstrue my words. Please, just forgive me this once. I will never transgress on my duties again."

"Tell me who you gave Chuko's destiny."

"I cannot tell you."

Edion's jaws clenches. "You will be locked in the dungeon of purgatory."

Agbavwo gasps. "My Lord Eternal, you belittle me by placing me in a cell with mere mortals."

"You erred lower than a mortal. Many centuries ago, I cast out your father onto the triangular earth because of a treasonable offence. You are a miniature of your father's peculiarity. Your blood will need to run on a crisscross vein to avoid the trait of your father. Agbavwo, you will atone for your unruly act in the den of purgatory and that is final. Your father is exciting enough havoc on earth. Do not rob me off the armistice to finding a solution to that. Be gone, you know the way."

Edion shakes his staff and the lid opens, two little pythons fly out and clasp Agbavwo's wrists. He disdainfully walks away. In purgatory, the humans are surprised to see an angel amongst them. They whisper to one another and steal glances at Agbavwo. He clenches his teeth in irritation and sits in a dark corner.

There is a large feast to celebrate Erin's birth. As Edion presents him to the deities, there is a heavy rumble in the cloud, which effectively rocks the earth, and there is a heavy thunderbolt in Igowe.

Edion puts Erin in a crib. He kisses his cheek and proudly sits on his throne. The deities come forward, bow and bear gifts to Erin, received by the goddess of fertility. They dance and make merry until the cloud turns golden.

Chapter Two

Igowe and Gwons will combat for supremacy. This battle is a decider on which kingdom will possess Egwolom-a goldmine in the borderline of their territories for the next hundred decades. In a sacred grove, the kingdoms' warriors gather to decide a setting for the war.

A guest chief priest from another land performs the rite of dipping a purple prediction cowry into a calabash filled with limewater for ten minutes. He washes the cowry until it turns white, cleans it with cotton, and then places the cowry on a lavender bed. Afterwards, he leaves the arena in rotating steps.

The priests from Gwons and Igowe respectively step forward. They polish the cowry with black and gold colour. A rocket lightening from the sky breaks the cowry into two-the gold and black pieces.

The priest of Gwons puts the cowries inside a dark hourglass and bows. They turn to the warrior camp of Igowe and both gestures for any warrior to come forward and pick a cowry.

Omena, the head warrior walks towards the stage but Keme stops him. Omena questioningly stares at Keme's hand on his arm. Keme slowly shakes his head, his smoky eyes softly beg for cooperation. Omena shrugs but Keme holds him firmly.

While Keme is five inches tall and broad-shouldered with hands surefire to effortlessly lift a battle-axe and kill ten people with a swing, Omena is six inches tall and has a wide chest, sinew arms, shoulders and hands that can masterfully wield a sword to go for the kill. Both are great warriors, but Omena can hold Keme down any day.

Omena tells Keme to allow him play the cowry, but Keme is adamant. Keme boasts that his luck will shine best.

"Omena, please grant me the honour of picking the cowry."

"Don't be stupid, Keme. You are thwarting my position. I am the head warrior. It is my duty to pick the prediction cowry."

Keme's high cheekbones come very close to his eyes, "I know, cousin, but…"

Omena grits his teeth, "formally address me as your superior. This is not a family meeting. It is an accession ceremony for the people of Igowe."

"Olorogun please let me pick the cowry."

Maduve comes to them, "what is going on here? The priests are waiting."

"Maduve, please take Keme away."

"Who will pick the prediction cowry?" The priest of Igowe irritably asks. He shakes the bracelets on his wrists, the hourglass glistens in darker hues.

"I am the one, oh, wise one," Keme says quickly and rushes at the priests.

Omena and Maduve step backwards and join the other warriors to watch. Omena balls his fists in anger.

The priest of Gwons holds up his wand and Keme stands still, "This is not a gathering of pigeons but eagles." He says. "Don't come too fast. Walk like a warrior that achieved a great feat on a bloody battlefield."

Keme is released from the spell and he grandly stride towards the priests. They part to give him access to the lavender bed. Keme deeply inhales and exhales, he stands at ease and magically dips his hand into the hourglass. He twists his hand for a while and smiles. He closes his eyes and sighs.

Omena lifts up his face to the cloud. His face rims with hope that Keme picks a favourable cowry, his shiny black eyes seem to have the stars missing in the cloud at daytime. Keme brings out his hand, his palm clasp around a cowry. He marches slowly to the priests. They nod. He opens his hand to the dark cowry. The prediction cowry reveals the Dark Angel Triangle will be the centre for the war.

Omena sees Keme's expression and comes to stand in front of him, "Keme, I should never have allowed you pick the cowry."

"I trusted my prediction; my instinct told me to make the pick. I had reassurance it would be in great favour of our kingdom. I thought I would pick the golden cowry. My instinct told me we would war closer to Igowe, on a plain."

"Assured by whom? Step aside, Keme. I am disappointed in…"

"Are you disappointed in me?"

"No, Keme. I am highly disappointed in myself." Omena strides to the chief priests and bows.

Keme awkwardly walks to them and kneel besides Omena. He presents the cowry to the priest of Gwons, "the fate of the battlefield has been decided. We will war at the Dark Angel Triangle."

The warriors of Gwons jubilate, clamping hands and hitting chests against chests.

"The gods are our witnesses," the priest of Gwons says. He receives the cowry from Keme and puts it in his ostrich medicine bag.

Omena and Keme rise. Other warriors tootle and beat their chests. They file out of the sacred grove. The chief priests sprinkles Holy water in the sanctuary and they simultaneously depart in backward movement.

Chapter Three

Igowe is a terrain with hills, mountains and rocks. It has a wild mangrove swamp forest. In the deep forest of Igowe, lies the savannah body that receives any ill-starred citizen, condemned to rot. The rivers link up to one another. There is a network of cleared and bushy paths linking towns and villages within and outside Igowe.

Omena sharpens his cutlass and thinks about how Igowe can defeat their opponent. Gwons is the devil's legendary kingdom because it is close to the Dark Angel Triangle. The war may be in their favour because it will be easier for them to regain weapons from their arsenals, unlike Igowe that will be miles away from home.

For generations, the cowry has favoured Gwons. Their luck outshines every other nation's wishes, and this makes them saber-rattlers. They always drive nations to their temper's extreme so that they urge to retaliate with might and strength.

The gods, of course, having no will to stop the foolhardiness of human creations, let them battle at loggerhead and scoff at their stupidity. Edion has made the Dark Angel Triangle the major host of war so that battles will look unattractive, but the warriors are daringly courageous and will step on the devil's tongue. Most nations have pleaded for the gods to extinguish the Dark Angel Triangle, Edion has promised to see to their prayer request but he is yet to conclude.

Keme walks into Omena's courtyard, "Omena."

"What are you doing here?" Omena says without looking at him.

"I came to say sorry. Omena, I am sorry."

"What prompted you to do what you did? The other warriors are blaming me for our woe."

"It was a bold instinct. I am so sorry about the outcome. I feel it will be of good. The premonition will manifest in the war with Gwons."

"Keme, are you insane? I pray one of us returns to tell our people how the war panned out. I cannot help but think you will be that coward. Please, leave my presence. I am busy."

"Omena, I am sorry. Please forgive me." Keme goes down on one knee, "I am sorry. We are great warriors. Other nations might not be a match for Gwons, but we might defeat them. Jar up leader. Jar up." Keme shakes Omena's thigh.

"Okay, you can go," Omena continues to sharpen his cutlass.

"There is one more thing," Omena looks up, "the dance. Maduve and the others are waiting for us. Let us have fun tonight as if it would be our last. But I am positive it will not be."

"I am not interested, there is a war brewing. I need to map out strategies which will get us out of the mess you created."

"Oma is back from her maternal village." Omena surprisingly looks up. "Yes, she will be at the dance. I saw her on my way here. She asked me to give you a message." Keme gives Omena a bracelet made with a blue yarn.

Omena drops the cutlass. He wears the bracelet and smiles.

"Now he is blushing. I will set your golden embroidery, go, and freshen up for the dance festival." Omena nods and leaves still blushing. Keme grins and follows him.

Maidens are dressed in their most fashionable attires to celebrate the dance. The arena is bursting with maidens and male peerage. Burning arrays of lit lanterns give the night a warm and flickering glow as strings of female dancers, thrill the crowd with their expertise in Ikebabi dance.

As they sexily wriggle alluring waists and clap their dainty feet on the ground, cheers, compliments, admiration, and whistles for more bodily gesticulation magic come from men, intrigued by their performances. The thoughts of most men centre on how to get them to wriggle the waists in their homely courtyards as wives.

A woman dancer is delectably twisting her waist in front of her dance partner, who holds on and guide the swings of her voluptuous buttocks, to sonorous beats of music played by some young men with flute and bands.

"Let us go from here and have our moments," Oma says to Omena who is tapping his feet to the rhythm of the music.

A tree branch shaped like an umbrella shadows a couple; their sexual movements are obvious as their bodies are plastered in a copulating position. The wild, steady back and forth movement of the man shows they are on passion for each other.

The man raises his woman's leg for deeper penetration. Oma clamps her thighs firmly to quench her sexual feelings. She grows envious of their tête-à-tête and wish to be in the arms of Omena, whose attention is on another swaying couple that are jamming into each other's bodies on the dance ground. Oma kisses him and takes his hand. She leads him away from the gathering and into the bush.

The moon is slim and thin shades of its lighting, provides cover for Oma and Omena as they forlornly walk through bush paths to a stream. An owl's shrieks give the night a sorcerous atmosphere. Omena carefully leads Oma to a river meant for female folks. As they pass a beautiful orchard, he gathers a handful of flowers. When they near the riverbank, Oma pulls her hand from his tender grip and willfully turns him around to face her. The flowers drop to the ground.

Oma rubs her full breasts on his obliging chest, "Let's stop beating about the bush. Take me Omena. As the war draws closer, my senses and imaginations are filled with your thrusts, I trust you will love me tonight."

He desirously caresses her arms, "Do you think I do not desire to take you with so much urgency, here and now?" He spans her waist with his sinew hands.

"Then show me how much you want me. I want to chant your name when I cum this explosive sweetness other girls giggle about in this stream. I do not want you to war. Love me always." She caresses his manhood through his golden lion skinned wrapper. Omena inhales deeply and closes his eyes.

"But Oma I must fulfil our ancestors' call. From the war, I may go astray to a world of no return."

"Omena, you planned to take me as wife within the eleventh market day, which is five days from now."

"That was before we were summoned to go to war with Gwons."

Oma hugs him, "Oh, you daredevil of mine…Then we can get married before your departure. Have an everlasting taste of me. Omena, I am thirsty for you. The consummation of our love will quench my longing."

"And one taste of you is insatiable. It will make me burn forever in longing. I always want to drink from every cup on your body. I do not want to leave you as a widow; I cannot bear you mourning all your beautiful years away while I may rot in an unmarked spot. I shall not take you for indefinite keeps and stop another from stably doing so." Omena caresses her arms and searches her eyes for understanding.

Oma rests her head on his chest and looks up to him, "It doesn't matter, if that ever happens; I know you've forever left a part of you in me. It would be like a waterfall in my soul. I want to feel the love from your eyes when you plunge me for the first time, or maybe the last time, leave your soul in me."

"I may leave you with child. You will become a mockery in Igowe; whole of the kingdom will call you an embarrassment to womanhood."

"There is no disgrace in love, only fools fall in love. I am spell bound to this stupidity to bed you. Take me and forget about the consequences." Omena tries to speak… She puts a finger on his lips, "Say no more, and become a part of me."

Omena swings her into his arms with urgency and makes his way into the stream's shrub. He puts her down to sit on a large fallen tree and caresses her stomach through her wrapper, tied firmly from her bosom to her knees. He pecks her cheeks one after the other and traces each beads on her waist with his burning stare.

"Oma, I only wish you will not regret this on your lonely nights."

"Why will there be regrets…" She searches his passionate eyes etch with warmth and something possessively savage.

"Oma, it's because I'll be gone for many nights..."

"When you come back, all my lonely nights will finally be over."

Omena shuts his eyes and pray for that possibility as he ponders, he may not be with her forever. He opens his eyes and exhales. He slowly lowers Oma on the tree.

He pours a handful of roses on her stomach. He spreads the roses on her stomach and drops kisses on her shoulders. He dips his tongue into her ear and whispers. Being pleased with her soft whimpers for more, he comes upon her and bites her ear slowly.

"Ouch," she is scared of his aggressiveness and tries to get up but he holds her shoulders down.

"It is too late to withdraw your consent. Oma, I am so hot for you, my innards burn for your softness. I can lose my mind if I do not love you tonight. Ease, my love; I'll be gentle with our love."

His calm eyes reassure Oma of his true feelings and she relaxes. They kiss passionately, unfasten each other's clothes, and make beddings with the clothes.

"Omena, do not go for the war, stay and let's make love forever."

The impossibility of what Oma said to him makes Omena position his body over hers and gives her deeper loving.

Her eyes widens, she pummels his back and thrashes her feet, "Ouch, Omena, what have you done?" She moans louder, "Omena, what have you done to me. Awww, it hurts."

"Oma, that is the feeling of love and war," he kisses her.

"No…" Oma beats his chest for him to get off her body but he holds her firmly with his whole body.

"To feel this love, you must first feel the pains like trolls of a gentle war. Relax, my love, the storm has passed. I shall pleasure you further. Ease, my love, okay?" Oma nods and pecks him on his forehead.

The wind carries sounds of their moans and groans to thatched roofs of the village occupants, that two lovers have consumed fruits of their love. An owl perches at a nearby tree, and peers upon the sated lovers like its preys with large forwarding eyes.

Omena retrieves his wrapper and uses it to protect them from the cold. He rubs her thighs and she strokes his chest. He kisses her lips and sits up. He unhooks his bracelet and puts it around her wrist, “Oma, this is a symbol of my love. Wear it always.” She pulls his face downward and kisses his forehead.

Oma wakes up and finds herself on an improvised bed of palm fronds. She remembers Omena had lifted her to get his clothing and dressed her up. She yawns and smiles wantonly. She heads home before it is fully dawn. The cocks crows loudly. She thinks her parent must not know she had not slept on her bed.

“May favour not despise our love, come back to me soon my love,” she smiles and wonders if Omena has reached the war front, she chants prayers as she hurries home. Her steps have bloomed from that of a maiden to a woman.

Chapter Four

The two nations go to war. Igowe warriors swim through an ocean while Gwons warriors only have to walk through a pond to get to the Dark Angel Triangle. The battleground is a dangerous narrow land in the centre of deep valleys. The land will barely accommodate the warriors, but all the warriors must fight on the plain.

Gwons and Igowe warriors stand at the two edges of the battlefield. They are drenched. Rays of sunlight shines upon the plains and dries up their bodies. The warriors begin to run towards one another, soon the warriors merges. They scream and charge to fight. There are clashes of steels and moans as men fall dead, howl as warriors takes on one another in a fiendish zest to earn victory.

In the upper world, Edion watches the battle between Gwons and Igowe. He stands up and all his angelic guards flank him. Edion is in a rage, the angels flap their wings to calm his nerves. He raises his arm and the mirror rotates.

The Dark Angel Triangle rotates violently and the warriors spin in confusion. Omena stamps his sword into the ground and digs his leg into the ground as well. A great wind whisks all the weapons away. The warriors are shocked.

"Foolish. After the war, their mothers and wives will cry to me over the loss of their men. Foolish men, they are foolish. In the aftermath of the war, their children will wail and wail and ask me Edion why, why Edion, oh, Edion why. No more weapons, no more war for today," the weapons appear at Edion's feet. He puts his arms down and the mirror becomes still.

The Dark Angel Triangle suddenly stops spinning. The warriors immediately unsheathe hidden daggers, clubs, and arrows. They continue the war with outlandish cries.

"My Lord Eternal, there is no retreat. They war still," an angel says.

Edion sighs and shakes his head, "Even the beasts have their own pleasantness; it only attacks trespassers in their domain. If a man abides by his hut, he would not have an encounter with the wild beast in a thick forest. The devil's sea sits on its own, the gods isolated it, yet the people always find a way to cross it and fly over it with spears and daggers. Let them be, I wanted to have some entertainment."

Edion takes his seat and watches the war. Some angelic guards stand at alert while others with their backs to Edion, surround the throne and flap their wings.

While Omena combats with several opponents, a Gwons warrior charges at him from the back. Omena jumps high and on a landing spree, he runs his sword on the necks of some opponents who groans and falls to the ground. He blocks a sword with his shield and rams his sword into the enemy's throat.

He quickly removes the sword and cuts off another's head. The enemy from the back run in faster pace, Keme kills a man and notices the Gwons warrior aiming at Omena with a dagger. Keme shoots his arrow at him, but he trounces the arrow with his dagger.

The Gwons warrior's face becomes menacing. Keme shouts Omena, but Omena is busy slashing and cutting bodies. Keme shouts Omena again, this time he hears him and turns around, an enemy cuts him serially. He sustains many injuries on his lower body.

Keme runs toward Omena, as the enemy plunges forward to strike Omena, Keme kicks his hand. He quickly crawls to pick up the dagger, Keme jumps and lands on his arm. The enemy screams in great pain and writhes on the ground.

Keme faces other combatants. The enemy agonisingly gets up and sneakily walks toward Omena, he lunges at Omena. Keme and Omena drive their swords into the enemy's heart.

A reinforcement army arrives from Gwons; they come in canoes, paddling wildly. They haul weapons to their army on the battleground and remain on the water. Gwons warriors smirk as they unsheathe their fresh swords. The lead warrior of Gwons licks the edge of his sword and grins at Omena. The fight continues. The battle is in Gwons favour, they are pressing the warriors of Igowe.

Most warriors of Igowe stand hopelessly. As they begin to retreat, giant snails rise from the valley. The snails mount one another to form a gigantic wall. This gives the warriors of Igowe time to gather strength and strike. The snails' shells melt any sword that hits it.

The lead warrior of Gwons recognises the defeat that awaits them and he furiously charges at Omena. Omena pose with his dagger but he is surprise the enemy ran to his back. He screams and cuts Omena from the back. Keme screams and kills the lead warrior of Gwons.

The people of Igowe rejoice. Women and children dance to the palace. The king bestows a vast estate and two big bags of gold to Omena, to other warriors; he gives small pouches of gold and portions of land. He pronounces Omena the greatest warrior of the nation. The people cheer Omena. He skilfully wields his sword, throws it in the air, jumps and catches it mid-air.

The king smiles and fans himself, "Today, I decree that no snail will ever be killed in Igowe. We shall no longer eat snails. They helped us during the war; therefore they shall be honoured in this nation." The people bob and clap.

Keme goes away from the palace arena. He enters his house and flings the bag of gold on the bed. The pieces of gold sprawl on the floor, he kicks the gold and it scatters around the room. He sits and rocks his chair back and forth. "It was my prediction that brought us this victory, yet Omena takes all the glory. He doubted my choice of cowry and now he reigns as the greatest warrior. He is given abundant rewards." Keme's eyeballs darken. He hears a knock on his door, he peeps through a slit in the window, and it is Omena standing at the door.

"Keme, are you home?" Omena knocks on the door. He comes by the window and Keme retreats. Omena knocks on the door again. He stands waiting for a response.

"I could swear I saw Keme walking home. I wonder why he left the arena without informing me." He shrugs and walks away.

Keme maliciously stares at him through the window. He kicks the chair and beat his chest as if he is beating a war drum. He hits his head on the wall several times. He rubs his forehead and stares at the blood on his hand. He grins.

The lovers stand under a tree. They are in tensed mood. Oma bends her head backward and dabs the corners of her eyes. She holds Omena's hands, "But you said you loved me, that you would marry me."

He pulls out his hands and shakes his head in agitation, "That was before the war."

She takes his hands again and places it on her chest, "Don't you feel the tempo of my heartbeats. Omena you are hurting me. What has changed? Omena, you promised marriage. You said we will carry out the marriage rites if you make it out of the war."

"My decision has changed," he drags his hands in exasperation and clenches his fist at his side.

Oma clamps a hand to her forehead; she wobbles, Omena tries to grip her but she shakes her head and put a palm on her ribcage. "I can't believe this. You break my heart so effortlessly. At least, tell me why you are discarding my love. Is it for another? Give me one reason. Omena, tell me the truth."

He looks away. "The words are difficult to say."

"Saying you won't marry me should have been the hardest statement.

But you uttered them easily."

"I cannot say it." He walks away. Oma stands awhile and runs to meet him.

She stands in front of him and spreads her arms, "I won't let you break off our engagement for no reason. You defiled my honour as a woman, Omena. Who will now marry me without questioning my virtue?"

Omena's cheeks quiver, "It was your decision Oma. You gave your pride willingly."

"And I've no regrets because I love you...that night was the best moment of my life. I feel you inside of me. Strongly I carry the passion of that night with me."

"Stop it, Oma. Do not recall the memories of that night. I cannot marry you and that's final."

She shakes her arms, "But Omena."

He places a finger on his lips, "Don't ask me for a reason. I cannot deal with it. I swear I cannot deal with it." He walks away in seething anger while she is distraught. She calls out his name and runs after him. She stands in front of him. "Get out of my way, Oma. Why will you not listen?"

"I won't until you tell why you will abandon me."

"Fine then, I will tell you." He stares angrily at her. He loosens his wrapper and Oma beholds his lost manhood. She gasps and moves backward. He joins his palms, "Now you can leave me in peace. In marriage, I shall be like your fellow woman. During the war, I lost my most prized strength as a man." He ties his wrapper and begins to walk away.

"Wait, Omena." he stops. "Your pride as a man lives in me." Oma takes his hands and place them on her stomach. "I'm carrying the seed of that night's harvest."

Omena leaps with joy. "Are you serious…Oma, please I hope I'm not dreaming. Just one night can result to this?"

Oma smiles, "A seed sowed in the night can bear much plant in the morning and bear fruits for centuries to come."

"Oma…Oh, I bless that night. The gods have shown me mercy." Omena hugs her tight, "but Oma, I will not be able to satisfy you. I will never be able to love you like I did that night." He looks sad.

"Don't worry Omena, we shall find other ways to explore sexual pleasure." Oma places her head on Omena's shoulder. He puts her hair in his face and breathes. He laughs happily. He gently twirls Oma and hugs her. She laughs happily.

Some maidens lead Oma to a newly built hut. It is time for the ritual of her marriage. The first step is to get Oma circumcised.

Ola, Oma's bosom friend rushes into the room. She pants and holds her waist, "Oma, I hope I have not missed any of the rituals. My parents have granted me permission to be your attendant. My lovely opha, I will be with you before your circumcision ceremony and after the marriage."

Oma hugs Ola and they giggle.

They dress Oma in beautiful red attire decorated with golden beads.

A young girl comes in, "Good day my ladies, Omena has sent this," she presents a little box.

Ola takes the box and opens it. She gasps.

"Ola, what is in it?" Oma asks.

"Gold, pure Gold, Oma," she says.

Oma stands up and looks into the box. She covers her mouth.

"Omena requests that your ceremonial attire should be adorned in gold." The girl runs away.

The maidens grin with envy. They chatter as Ola spread the gold in different trays. They attach it to Oma's dress.

A woman brings African red sandalwood. She smiles and caresses Oma's face, "Oma, when you left my house. I never imagined I would be coming this soon to perform your marriage rites. My sister would be so happy in the world beyond. Omena brought gold for you. He must love you so much."

Oma blushes. Her aunt rubs the substance on her face, "this beauty treatment shall cleanse your face and body. When I am done, you will glow like gold. This will leave your skin smooth, supple and shining for your husband to be. He will go mad with need when he holds you on your bridal bed."

All the maidens blush. Some of the girls sing and dance to entertain Oma.

"Aunt Umota, where is my cousin? I do not see Madu anywhere."

"He is busy with fishing. He will be on time for your marriage. He will not miss it for anything. He said he wants to catch giant fishes. He is going to personally grill the fish and serve your wedding guests."

"Awww…that is so sweet of Madu. He is the best cousin ever. He is an impressive young man."

"Yes, and let me go and see my own brother. I miss my brother-in-law, Kerhi." She pats Oma's cheeks and leaves.

In Gwons, Madu stubbornly pulls the boat forward and sail into the teeth of a storm in a river near the Dark Angel Triangle. The wind suddenly shifts and heavy waves hit the side of his boat. He holds the paddles down and braces for the hit. He kisses the necklace around his neck. Water engulfs him and he holds his breath. The velocity dies down and he begins to paddle the boat.

"This is a dangerous aquatic terrain. Only brave fishermen dare to fish in this sea. The first men caught by the mysterious ocean had gone fishing, daring to catch fat prizes. Their boat capsized and they drifted away to an unknown destination. Their families are still searching for them. Today, I dare this sea and I shall come out favoured." Madu says and paddles the boat with greater force.

Madu has promised to give Oma a fat wedding treat. He has come this far to cast his nets and hooks to fulfil his words. He stands and throws his net into the sea. The net sinks deeper and he smiles. He slowly drags the net forward. His muscles bulge. He catches different species of big fishes. He drops the catch in a big bowl of water and sail away with happy smile.

He docks in the riverbank at his backyard and ties the boat rope to a pole. He takes few strides into his compound. For his safe return, he offers sacrifices of thanks in his family shrine. He unties a fowl attached to a fishing hook. He slits the hen's neck with a small knife and spills the blood around the shrine. He cleans the knife on the fowl feather and places the knife in a pot.

Madu removes the necklace, hangs it on a feminine statue and bows to the smiling symbol of safety and luck. Afterwards, he sits and rests his back. He sees a seashell hanging on his clothe and removes it. He studies the beautiful white shell and kisses it.

After a while, Madu prepares a cart for the journey to Igowe. Some of his neighbours assist him to put the bowl of fish in the wagon.

In the groom ritual ceremony, some of the warriors make Omena sit on a low bronze stool. Keme and Maduve apply camwood powder on his arms and face.

"Don't rub it all over my body, men. I still have to do some sword practice and I also have a meeting with the king."

"It has to be all over your body, man. I command you to unwind and allow us perform this rite. If you cannot endure this, you should not have proposed to Oma." Omena laughs and his body jiggles. "Be brave warrior. The women are busy with their preparations. We do not want to be late, no real groom keeps a bride waiting," says Maduve.

"Cut it out, Maduve. I really do not like the feel of this powder on my face," Omena rubs it off.

"Then you have to pay in order to avoid the powder being all over your body. We are not having mercy on you." Keme says.

"Yeah, yeah," Omena gives Keme a bag of gold coins, "share the token with one another and stop pampering me like a princess." The warriors laugh. They play flute, drink wine and do some wrestling contest.

Madu arrives. He stoops and hugs Omena, "I am in time for the real fun, brother-in-law."

Omena pats his back, "Ah, Madu, I am glad you came. Oma's heart will leap in joy."

"Not as high as you make her heart leap. I could hear her heart beating to the rhythm of your love. She did not wait to attend my birthday party when she heard you were going to war. I should not be congratulating you on defeating my kingdom and denying me of striking gold. But, congratulations brother, I am happy for you and Oma. Love my Oma, always."

"Thanks, Madu. Trust me, I will."

Madu winks at him and retreats, "where are you going," asks Omena.

"I have a feast to prepare. There will be grilled fish at your wedding reception. All your guests have to do is point at any fish of their choice; I will kill and grill a tasty morsel." Madu rubs his palms in delight. The men cheer at the yummy preparation and Omena laughs. Madu chuckles and leaves.

They get married and Oma bore triplets, a girl and two boys. For three years, they live in peace with love, patience and understanding.

Omena practices sword moves in his private courtyard. His sword is thick-backed and weighted with bronze with its tilt flashing with gold. Oma brings him a cup of water. She admires his dexterity of combating the carved opponents. It feels like she is witnessing a real battle.

She smiles, "Have a break, I brought you some water."

"How did you know I was thirsty," he kisses her and takes the cup of water.

"You have been in here for three hours."

He gives her the cup, "what else do you have for me?"

"Nothing, but you have something for me," she drops the cup on a table. Oma takes a double-edged sword from his wall of fame.

"Oma, please handle it with care. It is not one of your kitchen knives." Omena wields his sword.

"Teach me how to fight," she holds the sword and points it at him.

"Why should I, my lady?"

"Because, when you go out to war, I will be in charge. In case the enemy attacks our home, I will be able to defend our children and myself."

He nods, "but I will not teach you for free."

"Name your price; I will pay you in gold."

"You will pay me back with my own coins?"

"Okay, I will pay you in bed. We will have a lovers squabble on the bed."

"I have already paid your kindred for that power you will wield against me. I own all you have. You're my possession."

Omena changes his sword. "Let us do this; you will act like a slave that needs to fight her master to regain her freedom."

"But there is no chance of me winning you."

"We will battle for five nights; I will train you to match my prowess. Jar up warrior princess. Prepare for combats."

Oma poses her sword and grins. Omena shows her ways to handle a sword. Omena rushes forward and clanks her sword. Oma stares in shock, "do you want to kill me Ome…"

"I am your Lord and Master. Your opponent, be ever ready to take on your enemy. Now, fight," he shouts and scrapes the tilt of his sword on

Oma's blade.

She jerks up her sword and pants. He rushes at her and she quickly repels his attack, their swords cross. Oma bends down and spins her sword and Omena jumps up to escape the cut.

He raises an eyebrow, "Where did you learn to fight like that?"

"My father taught me that."

"He showed you how to fight with fishing nets and hooks?"

"No, with hoes and cutlasses," Oma kicks his hind and grabs his balls. He bends on one knee and she places the sword on his chin.

"He taught you to fight with hoes and cutlasses, right? Your sweet hole will pay for this tonight."

She bends towards him and says, "I can't wait."

He kisses her, "my love, be patient my warrior queen. It would be a fierce battle."

Keme comes in, "wow, wow, I am sorry. I didn't know the sword ground has turned into your private chamber." Oma disengage from the lovers' position and drops the sword, "greetings Oma."

Oma smiles shyly, "Greetings to you Keme. We did not hear you come in. How long have you been here?"

"I came in when Omena kissed you."

Oma blushes, "I will get you a drink," She takes the cup and hastily leaves.

"Lover warrior, time to get up," Keme says and gives Omena a hand to get up.

"What brings you?"

"I am just from the king's palace. I think we are set to go to war."

"We are to war with who?"

"That is undisclosed."

Omena hangs the swords. He admires his collection of gold and bronze swords. "I cannot wait for the war. I wonder what bounty the king will reward us with when we come back victorious."

"I see the gold is not enough for you."

"Keme, this present gold is nothing compared to the wealth I will amass in the future." Keme eyes him contemptuously. "I will build grand empires before my princes and princess comes of age. I need to shower."

"Yes, you are sweaty. Have a good scrub. I will take my leave. Please, tell your wife I will have the wine next time."

"I will." Keme nods and leaves through the courtyard door. Omena goes to have his bath.

Oma serves Omena's meal and put it in his parlour. She goes to call him from the garden behind the kitchen.

Omena eats the meal. He falls to the floor, his eyes bulging. He clamps his hands around his throat and coughs. His eyes are watery. He groans and crawls toward the door, blood gush from his mouth. He dies as Oma steps in. She screams and falls on him.

Two days after Omena's burial, his sons fall ill and die of an adulterer curse. In grief, Oma pleads to Omena's kin she is not guilty of the accusations that are levelled against her. The way Omena coughed blood is the way a husband dies when his wife has had an affair with another man. She swears she did not have sex with another man.

A week later, she gets permission to come out of the mourning room. She goes to her house to get some clothes and sees Keme rummaging Omena's trunk. She quietly backs off and peeps at him. Keme takes a portrait of Omena. He lifts it to his eye level and stares in disgust. He throws it on the floor, stampede on the paper sketch with his feet and spits on it.

Oma gawks open-mouthed. She confronts Keme and boldly tells him he has a hand in her misery. She grabs his shoulders and shakes him, "You weren't happy when Omena was proclaimed the greatest warrior of Igowe, and also the massive land the king gifted him, and it pained you to the bones. Therefore, you killed him to gain all his wealth. But why, he regarded you as his own and shared almost everything with you. Keme, did you have to kill your own because of these diminishing worldly possessions?"

He pushes her. Oma hits her back against the wall. She winces and rubs her back. Keme closes the trunk and picks up the sketch. He dusts it and put it in the trunk.

"You don't know what you're talking about." Keme is surprised at her calculations and becomes furious. "Oma, you have swallowed a cassava ball too big to go down your throat. You accuse me falsely. It will bring the end of you. It will choke you."

"Perhaps I have swallowed a big ball of cassava, but there is still space in my throat to enable me voice out your evil deeds to the elders. Keme, your threats are empty."

"Oh, I see."

"Yes! Keme, I promise you. You will pay for my husband and sons' death."

"Too many talks…Oma, let me see you try." In his mind, Keme vows to ruin her before she overrides him. He thinks of disclosing how Omena had lost his reproductive organ before he married Oma to his kindred. He smiles, thinking how easily this revelation will crush Oma and her willful spirit to expose him.

Oma is feeding her daughter when the elders call her. She curtseys, "My elders, I greet you all."

The eldest kinsman says to her, "Oma, please stand in the middle of this gathering."

Oma looks at the unsmiling faces of the elders. She sighs and steps sluggishly to the centre with folded arms. Her feet points towards him.

Her daughter walks toward her crying. Oma opens her arms and the child embraces her. She stops crying after Oma fusses over her. Her daughter sits on the floor. She sucks her thumb and move closer to Oma's feet. Oma looks down and plays with the beads on her waist.

The eldest kinsman points to her daughter, "Oma, that child at your feet, who is her father?"

Oma jerks her head. "I beg your pardon." She kneels and hugs her daughter.

"Do you need the feathers of a white cock to clean your ears before you can hear me, or I should place my mouth in them and speak louder? I asked who fathered this girl, and the boys that perished after Omena's death."

Oma looks at Keme and he grins at her. There are no crinkles around his eyes. "Omena, my late husband fathered the children." All the elders start murmuring at once. Oma wrings her hands.

"May we have some silence please?" They stop talking. "Oma, you may not want to tell us the father, or fathers of the children, but please do not stain the memory of our late brother and son."

"I bore fruits formed by my husband's seeds!" she sighs and talks calmly, "My elders, if the children are not his, why did Omena acknowledge them as his. And the curse you people said killed my sons, why did it become effective if the children are not of his loin." Her daughter crosses her arms and legs. She kicks her foot and sucks her middle finger.

Keme says, “Perhaps he was blind and of course, stupidly in love with a cheap woman as you.”

“Keme, don’t you dare, don’t dare soil my name you wretched evil man.”

Keme shrugs, “Do you have a name? Your name is already buried.”

Oma points a warning finger at him…

An elder stops her before she speaks. “Eh, keep quiet; you do not point fingers at a man. Put those weak hands to order or they will be chopped off.”

Oma slowly put down her hand. Tears rolls down her cheeks and drops on her daughter’s head. She clutches her beads.

“My elders, you see how wild her tongue is. Oma, just tell the elders the truth. Save us all these drama. I’ve already confided to my clan, that since the last war, Omena was without manhood.”

“Yes Oma, tell us how you got pregnant by a man that had no manhood.” An elder says.

Oma pants heavily, she could not defend how she got pregnant out of wedlock. For that night of passion, the village will still banish her from the land. It is a taboo for a girl to lose her maiden head before marriage. The laws are strict. She keeps quiet for her daughter’s sake; she cannot be away from her or take her through dangerous terrains searching for a new settlement.

The eldest kinsman speaks, “You will go in and pack your belonging, since you cannot give an answer to this honourable clan. There is no question if any of our kinsmen will inherit you as a wife because you are not fit to remain in our family."

Oma's legs shudder, her lips quivers and her eyelids dilates. "Your judgement is harsh on me. I promise you all, I'm innocent." She caresses her daughter's chin, "this is Omena's child."

"Oma, you're a disgrace to womanhood." Keme says and spits on her face.

The eldest kinsman shouts, "That is enough Keme. Oma, you can go and take this girl along to your father's house. She is not of our flesh and blood." Oma closes her eyes in sorrow and wipes off the spittle. "Did you not hear me? I said, take your daughter and be gone from this household."

"No, the girl will stay with us," Keme blurts.

"Keme, no part of this disgrace will be left in our family. I have spoken. That is my final decision. I hope I have made a wise judgement to savage our clan's honour." The clansmen nod in approval.

Oma cries as she packs her belongings. She looks at the house they had shared so many memories. The happy and sorrowful moments makes the teardrops intensify.

Keme comes in unnoticed. "I told you. I now have the last laugh."

"You have shamelessly caused restlessness for Omena. I could take the slander on my person, but you extended it to my children and husband. Why did you do this?"

"You stepped on my toes so hard. Crushing you harder was the only way my mind will find appeasement. I love this sorrowful tears swimming in your eyeballs."

"Not only tears should you see, but the pain you've caused me in my heart. You can have this miserable joy as much as it pleases you. Move out of my way." Keme steps away from the door and Oma walks out with her daughter.

As they walk away, Keme thinks he should keep Omena's daughter under his watch. She may be a threat to him in the future. He turns around and Oma is gone from sight. He spits. He cleans his lips with an arm, "The elders do not understand why this child must be under my watch. She may come back to haunt me. I see her mother's spirit in her eyes, and she possesses Omena's strength." He says quietly.

He quickens his steps to catch up but decide to go with some men. He turns around and veers off a bush path. He comes upon some gaunt looking men who are playing board games. One player to another thumps the stones into the wooden board.

Keme coughs. They stand fast and bow. He slowly walks towards them and topples the board game, "there is a serious task to do."

The cart Keme is riding raises dusts. He rides faster to catch up on Oma. The cart draws abreast of her. He jumps out of the buggy and one of his men takes the reigns and slows down.

He takes the child from Oma. She grabs her child and put her astride her waist but Keme wrestles the child out of her arms with his greater strength. The toddler cries to be back in her mother's arms.

"Don't take my daughter away from me. She is the only one I have."

"My cousin's child will not be bred by a characterless woman."

"Oh, now, you agree she is your cousin's child? I thank the gods for this admittance."

He puts the child down, "Oma, you now have the floor to frolic with your numerous lovers."

"Keme, you've tarnished my dignity. The accusations you heaped on me are all false. I wonder why the elders believed you so easily. But I get it now; you and your kindred are in this together."

He slaps her. There is blood on her lips, "You insult the elders of my clan? Now I see you have gone mad. I fear it is infectious. I don't want my cousin's child to contract this disease." He drags the child's hand, "come my dear. We will go to your aunt. My wife will be a good mother to you." The child bites his thumb and Keme yowls, "stop that you little witch and come with me."

He lifts her into his arms. Oma struggles to get her child and bites Keme on his wrist. He grits his teeth and blows her chest. The child is crying and thrashing her hands towards her mother while Keme's henchmen hold her down.

"Come back with my child Keme. You vile man, don't take my child away from me." Oma punches and bites the men.

The henchmen let go of Oma after Keme rides off with her daughter in the cart. Two men rolls a big rock out of the bush, they run off as Keme whips the horse to run faster. A wheel pulls out of the cart. Oma sees Keme flinging her daughter out with great force. The little girl rolls and hit her head on a big rock. From a distance, Oma holds her head and screams. She faints. Rain begins to fall, the droplets on her face awakens her. Oma begins to roll and kick her feet on the wet ground.

"Ah, Keme, Keme taking my husband and sons was not enough for you. Keme, you have taken my last child as well. Oh, the god of vengeance will visit you. He shall ravage you with a fiery thunder never seen in Igowe. Oh, god of vengeance, someone has gravely wronged this woman. Give justice. Please, mete out justices upon my assailant." She cries in anguish and calls upon the god of vengeance.

The god of vengeance is at his dinner when his vengeful staff vibrates, the head of the staff burns brightly. He wants to ignore the call for vengeance until after he has his meal, but the sorrowful cry of a woman distracts him. He stands before the gigantic mirror of Ikumodo and watches what troubles her.

It has stopped raining. Oma lay on the cold ground, crying for her daughter to come back to her. It has been long a woman sought his intervention. Most of the women in the kingdom could handle their own problems. The men usually call out silently to him in their hearts. On this rare occasion of hearing a woman's turmoil, leaves him in disarray of a burning vengeance. He reviews the ills done to Oma. Through her eyes, he sees that Oma senses Keme have wiped out her husband's entire generation so that none of them will contend their father's properties.

Oma's eyes become very tearful, and Erin could not see the depths of the events that have taken place. He turns to the other side of the great mirror for clarification. Keme poisoned his cousin's dinner in order to acquire his landed properties and gold.

Oma's cries almost move him to tears but he dried his watery eyes with the magic of Uriadam. A drop of his tears can cause flood all over the kingdom.

"Igowe has never seen such greed, jealousy and intense wickedness. I wonder why Keme is still walking this earth freely. I've to tell the god of karma that he is too slow with his law of retributions." His eyes become red. Erin wants to avenge Oma's pains, face to face with her assailant. His rage boils when he replays how Keme's henchmen had crushed her to the ground.

He spits out the soup in his mouth, the force split the cloud and particles fall to the earth. He sends back his meal to the goddess of harvest. The goddess of harvest grabs the meal with her huge hands. She looks at the food and her fat jaw drops, and then she spins it into purgatory. The souls in purgatory rush at the food and eat with delight.

Oma's predicament has filled him with a vengeful appetite and he starts wielding thunder. He flexes his muscles and exercises his feet. Erin is benevolent and malevolent to human beings.

He could not resist any grave injustice that triggers his temperament. Erin forcefully clamps his hands. He rotates and invokes instant lightning bolts with loud thunderclap. The sun and moon stand still in their habitation, as the tilts of his arrows split the cloud, and at the glittering bolts, the people of Igowe marvels at such rear sight.

The people fear an instantaneous and retributive destruction on their nation. They wonder who have greatly offended the god. As his staves continuously cut through the sky, the lightening closes in like a whirlwind to toss Igowe into a terrible condition. The people in loud plea ask Erin to spare their lives and properties. Erin's anger subsides, he pants and red sweat gathers on his arms. The people raise their hands towards the sky in gratitude.

Oma is gravely ill. The rumble in the rain has left her feverish. Kerhi set fire to Osurhomu-a lamp to preserve Oma's life. He carries the hurricane lamp and positions it in the centre of her room. He always refuels to ensure it never goes off. No matter how wounded Oma is, she stays alive if the lamp does not go off, her breath pumps up as long as the fire is on.

After days of treatment, Oma is not healing. She begs her father to put off the lamp as her health deteriorates. She does not want her father to go on suffering by tending her in his old age.

"Father, please, let me go to the gods. It is a mockery for a father to do this for his child. Why has the gods mocked us so. Put an end to this misery. I do not want to see you suffer any more. Tending me day and night will make you weaker and sick. Father, you might die." Tears roll down her cheeks.

Her father massages her feet with ointment. "Do you want to die before your old father? It took your mother and me many years to conceive. The gods blessed us with a beautiful soul, and it was you my daughter, Oma. I lost your mother during your birth. I do not want to lose you during health trials. I will keep you alive. That is all I want. Your death shall be transferred to me, any cost to keep you alive, I'll do it."

"No, no, not you father. Let me go. I want to join my husband and children."

He soaks thick cotton in a bowl of steaming water. He winces at the hotness and squeezes the cotton. He uses it to massage her abdomen. Oma screams and flips her back.

"I did not know you were this selfish. Did you think it was easy living without your mother? I wanted to go with my wife, but I chose to stay with my child. Oma, after I die, you can go. But for now, leave me to do what I want. Let this old man go in place of you if need be."

"Please, don't, father. I want you to go away from this room."

"Then who else will come to care for you? Who else comes close to you in this period of your sickness? When this sudden attack came on and you started showing signs of death, many people ran away from us. The people are no longer encouraged to see you, at a time like this; Igowe's tradition does not encourage team love. They have offered to take turns and work on our farms while I tend you, which is the least help they can give. I pray the gods bless them with bountiful harvests. I'll give up my life to end this misery."

"No, father. Do not say that."

"I'll my daughter. Because I cannot bear when married women, younger than you in age will come with a short piece of plank and pair of bamboo along with clappers to sing and dance over your corpse. I know Oma, your dead ears, will not hear the songs, I will be the one to listen to it all and it will eventually kill me. Let me die, so that they come to perform in my room. Let this be my own rite to final passage. Before you I came, before you I shall go. It is a shame for a child to die before a parent. Who will bury me if you die? Let me go and offer sacrifices for your life to get redemption. I shall go to the deep forest and find a source of life. I will be successful. Our ancestors are with me. Their children have always buried them, mine will not be different."

"But what is the essence of living, everything has been taken away from me."

"I'm here."

"But I'm a burden to you. I should have been the one to take care of you while the hurricane lamp burns so that I can preserve you to see my children's children. If your grandsons and granddaughter were alive, they would have been able to tend you. They would have preferred to set a healing balm at the back of the house for your wellness and preservation. I want this to discontinue."

He strokes her hair, "I will preserve your life because you can still give me more grandchildren. Through you, I will have a long line of descendants. Let me try another medicine, maybe both of us can be saved." Oma nods and weakly pats her father's hand atop her head.

Kerhi goes to his personal shrine. He drinks palm wine and sprays it on the ancestral objects in the grove. He chants some indigenous prayers and heads to the forest. He picks up a dried shiny red leaf-the food Erin had thrown down to earth.

He holds his waist and uses cutlass to trim tree branches to wade his way out of the bush. He gets home, boils the leaf amongst other herbs, and gives Oma to drink. She holds the cup in shaky hands and drinks slowly. She coughs and hands the empty cup to Kerhi.

"Oma, the light of the lamp will not stop shining, it will burn forever more." He looks up to the roof, "the ears of my ancestors hear me now, fill my anguish with respite, my faith in you is overflowing. If you do not save my child, the voice of adoration from my child and I will no longer call upon your name, broken hands cannot pour libations and torn tongues cannot honour your name. Show us mercy, that we have not been fools for serving you every day. Save my daughter. Oh, gods of our land, for an incessant religious observance to you save my lineage. Our ancestors were great devotees to you and we never wandered to seek help from sorcery of the dark underworld. I have tried all I can, please save my daughter."

Kerhi place his hands on her abdomen and press down until she vomit five tiny green stones. He tells himself to be calm and closes his eyes. As Oma regains strength, she feels a healing warmth surge through her body and the burning temperature of her eyes cool down. Oma is well again. Kerhi comes out of her room and lifts his face to the starring sky. Tears of joy fill his eyes. He happily walks to the shrine with a gallon of palm wine chanting words of praise to the gods.

Edion is busy at a ritual of conjuring images of all the kingdoms. He sees the happenings all over the earth. A man steals sacrificial offerings from a shrine. Edion shakes his head. As the thief is running, he kicks his leg on a thick rope, the rope cuts. A wide slim rock falls and splits his head. Edion sees another man helping his brother who is drowning in a river. He nods his head.

A woman begs a trader to give her food for her and her skinny children to eat. The tradeswoman gives the woman some pineapples, bush meat, cassava flour and palm fruits. The woman and her children kneel and thank the tradeswoman. After begging some other traders, she and her children go to another market to sell the items. Edion sighs.

He flips the mirror with a finger, he is satisfied with the cosmologies, and peers quirkily at his oncoming troubled son. Erin has come before his father to tell him his decision to relocate to earth. He bows, "Father, I will fall to earth for a while."

Edion raises his upper limb; two angelic guards hold his arms and help him to sit forward. They bow and let go of him then move backwards to their stations.

"Son, when did you arrive at such an important decision?"

"Few minutes ago, and I shall leave at once."

"You do not have my consent. Your place is here."

Erin walks towards the mirror and views the earth, "Father, my subject needs my utmost intervention. She is grieved stricken."

"You can atone her grieve to joy right here; you do not need to make your resolution in physical form on earth."

Erin folds his arms, "But other gods can."

"You're not other gods. You are my beloved son. You are the heir to my throne."

"Father, I know. But Oma needs me. It is a must I go."

"So that is her name." Edion plays with a golden ball, "Have you fallen in love?"

"I am not in love, I am duty bound to the mortal."

"Your heart is immortalised to love the mortal."

"I am not of flesh and blood."

"But you will be when you take on the human form."

Erin kneels, "Father, why the fuss. In the beginning, you sent the god of stream to earth without much hesitation, permanently for that matter. Mine is temporal, I shall be back."

"The stream deities were positioned on ground because the water needs to be on land to be near the people and depart for the rivers and sea when the temperature becomes hot in the dry season."

"I wish to be merged with the stream."

"That will never be possible. Erin, come to your senses. You will rule after me. You are my heir."

"I'm in my right senses. It is you father, who has taught that our duties should come before our personal needs, our fulfilment comes with the happiness of the mortals. I cannot bear the sufferings of Oma. It is evil to separate a child from the mother, worse, is killing the children of one woman." He crosses his arms on his chest and bows. "I pledge Keme shall feel my wrath. I will not spare him."

"Erin, what happens when other seekers of vengeance call upon you?"

"I shall give succour when I am on earth, to every beast and man, I am duty bound to fight their courses when they call upon me. Father, I think the god of karma falters in his duties. If he is proficient at dispensing quick judgements, I will have fewer calls from the mortals."

"I think he now does a better job. He is less lenient to erring earthlings," Edion recalls the fate of the thief in the shrine.

Erin folds his arms, "I hope he quickens judgement."

"So, will you be born of a woman? Will she be a virgin or a harvested tree?"

Erin shakes his head and prances gently. He taps his left wrist, "No, I shall storm the earth like a nomad. If I go as a baby, I will not have the strength to help Oma, and by the time, I am grown, the vengeance would be cold, I will avenge the ills without fierceness and that will be unfair to Keme's crime. I shall follow the stars of the South; it will lead me to my goal. I shall wait for a Good Samaritan to find me. My father, I've come to you, for your approval and blessings." Erin bows, "My Lord Eternal, please hewn me with unquenchable fire that my spirit for vengeance will burn alive and doesn't grow cold for vengeance."

"I hope it doesn't wane in love."

Erin frees his arms and bangs his chest, "It will burn whatever love and affection I have."

"I am worried."

"Do not be, father, I am the thunder god, my vengeance gives me this restlessness to fulfil my duties, my duty is bound to this throne, I shall be back."

"What makes you feel her call for vengeance is that serious? Erin, what if she is calling your name in vain?"

"Her veins are too weak to cry vain tears. The people of Igowe hardly take the names and duties of the deities for granted. Father, this is a true call. I am ever active and responsive in that if one does an evil and pretentiously invokes the name of god of thunderbolt and vengeance to exonerate him or herself, I will expressly send that person to purgatory without further trial. I think she is wise enough to know a reserved thunderbolt can kill any mischief-maker; it does not exempt any woman or child. My seekers must come with equity to seek justice over a fellow mortal that has lost his or her sanity of goodness."

"Accurately said, Erin, the birds do not fly above the heaven, and the fishes cannot swim on the surface of the water. Human beings do not see the state of their hearts when they grieve, but the deities engrave them in their mirror of obligations. She might have called out your name in vain. Send another deity to carry out this task. Or instruct karma to ruin Keme in an instant."

Fire rims Erin's eye pupils. "My Lord Eternal, I shall avenge this injustice, personally."

"Erin, stay in your place and carry out your duties."

"No father, I shall journey, for the fool speak and act iniquity, and my believers are dying for his vicious cowardice."

"When they whisper and mutter for us to come to their aid, they do not mean you should physically be in their midst. You can save Oma from here. You fight for them from afar, at dawn when their problems get solutions, they give testimony from afar, and we are content with our lots. What is this discontentment that drives you to the realm of mortals, Erin?"

"I'm Erin; you make me pass through fire in the valleys of fire and brimstone. I have amassed the skills of twirling thunderbolts, and wielding my sword of vengeance to destroy any dark sages of witchcraft, wizardry, sorcery and inhumane acts. No mortal provokes my anger to this extent and go scot-free, even other gods tremble at my reprisal when they outwit justice and fairness in their duties. Father, remember what your thunderbolts had caused before you became Lord Eternal. You had broken down when you saw the destruction you had caused the kingdom, and I was born to rebuild altars so that the heavenly kingdom will remain in existence to serve the needs of the world. I do not want to exert my anger here, the kingdom will perish. Please, let me go. I do not want to be a host of destruction in my father's kingdom. Let Keme feel my wrath directly."

"I warn you Erin, your name may be built in Igowe forever. I fear you will be erected as an altar in the shrine of Igowe."

"No father, I shall be back. I shall be back. I shall be back to reign."

Edion calls the wise men and sorcerers to foresee Erin's fate. They join their staffs and become white rhinos. The magicians strike their wands at the rhinos and whisk them away to consult the golden goblet of destiny.

Through the goblet, the rhinos foresee Erin in a threatening dilemma. The rhinos return and transform into the wise men. Edion gestures for them to tell what they saw. The wise men shake their heads. The sorcerers try with their arts to change the outcome of Erin's fate, but they could not. Edion bends his staff and strike the mist upon the cloud that it may become blur for Erin to see through. He looks gloomy and powerless to change his son's decision.

He creates a universe above the earth that Erin will only make out fireflies and beasts in it. Erin grows excited on seeing the bestial creatures. Edion hopes that soon, this omen of Erin going to earth to intervene for Oma will fade. All divinations have revealed a doom if he goes away. He sends Erin to the goddess of harvest to feed on iron and ore. As he eats, the goddess of harvest worries that the evil of the underworld's fire may hold him down forever and consume him.

Edion does not give him escorts to see him off to the river to have a bath of fortification and a change of skin. As Erin heads to the river, some souls in purgatory try to hold his garment and drag him in. He uses his palms to spray fire on their arms and increases his strides. Agbavwo sneers at him. Erin walks into a pool filled with lavender. He splashes water on his face. He inhales the fragrance of the flowers and dips the rest of his body into the water.

Erin returns. His complexion has become bronze. "I give you twenty-one days to accomplish your mission and return to the upper world, or else, you will cease to be a god," Edion says.

Edion pours cauldrons of fire into Erin. "Have enough of fire, so that your task shall be accomplished with ease. But I withhold the magical power, it absence will not make you hold long on earth. Even if you are tempted to stay, you shall not stray, you will not hold for long. You shall hurry back to be seated in majesty. Take this along." He gives Erin a silver cutlass.

Erin bows and takes the cutlass. He inserts it into a sheath at his back. Erin holds thunderbolts in his right hand and slams it to the cloudy floor, it rattles violently, and he rolls another bolt on his left hand and slams harder.

The earth reverberates. Children and adults in Igowe turn around. They run helter skater to get to huts. They wonder if the world is ending. They go in frenzy search for their loved ones. The trembling of the earth cease and they are dazed seeing one another alive, unscathed and whole.

The last thunderbolts have fragmented the cloud, and below, Erin sees the wilderness that awaits him. He does not turn around to look at his brooding father. Erin crosses his hands on his chest and jumps down.

Chapter Nine

Erin lands in a forest. At first, He finds disfavour in the wasteland. He smiles as he sees two squirrels running after one another. He walks towards the fighting animals.

"Stop right there. From which clan are you?"

He stops and turns around to see Kerhi. "I'm no son of Igowe. I am from a distant land. I've come, to build a new life in any hospitable village that welcomes my wandering feet."

Kerhi appraises him. "Yes, I see from the strangeness of your guided steps that you're a stranger, for any man that needs direction in his own house, has either become newly blind or he is an impostor."

"I know my home and the destination of my mission." He mutters.

"What did you say?"

"I would be pleased to have some water, my throat is dry, you see, I've been travelling from miles."

"Are you serious?"

"Yes, I am very serious."

"Come, walk with me. I shall give you hut and warmth in the village."

"I am thirsty."

"Yes, I shall give you water at home. I did not carry a water pot on my head from the fishing festival. I did not know I would come across a dehydrated traveller. Come, we should move fast, there has been an earthquake in the land. Did you feel it?"

"Yes, I did." Erin smiles over what his vengeful landing had caused.

"I feared we were all going to die. We shall offer a General Thanksgiving to Edion. Only the gods knows what would have been our fate if the earth had not stopped spinning."

"It was nothing of the sought; it was just a mere opening of the cloud and my landing."

"What did you say?"

"I said you should lead the way."

"Oh, okay, this way." Kerhi leads the way out of the bush.

Erin is glad that Oma's father welcomed him forehand to his mission and has given him shelter. He could not have guessed the outcome, because his omniscient power is not with him. As he walks behind Kerhi, Erin sidesteps the snails on the ground.

Oma lie on her back and watch the clouds go about its business for the evening. The night is gathering too quickly. She arises from the sleeping mat when she sees her father approach. She runs towards him, "Father, you took a long time coming back. I was startled by the earthquake and frightened over your well-being, and prayed to the gods to keep you safe and bring you back home." She hugs him and collects his farm tools. "Welcome father, I shall get you a cup of cool water to quench your thirst."

"My dear, make it two cups, I've brought a guest. His name is…"

Erin comes forward and places a hand on his chest, he bows slightly to his host without taking his intense stare off Oma. "My name is Erin."

"Oh, you share a name with the god." Oma says.

"I'm a shadow of a god."

"I pray you do not bring down our roofs with thunderbolts." Kerhi says and Erin smiles.

Oma's gaze locks with his, she sees something like glistering fire shine in his eyes. She shivers and looks away. Oma calls out hurried inaudible greetings to him and rush off to the back of the house. While she fetches cups of water from the big clay pot, she wonders what is in him that made her shiver.

After they drink some water, Kerhi goes into the kitchen. He drops his fishing tackles and nets on the ground, he hangs a basket full of fish and meat over a low burning fire, to keep the proteins dry.

"Father, next time I'll go to the fishing expedition with you." Oma says whimsically.

"You will stay back home and keep it clean and warm for my arrival.

Idjędę takes months or weeks. During the fishing festival, some of the fishermen up their games with hunting, and I don't want you caught up in any danger."

"Okay, if you say so."

"Yes, go and see that our guest is comfortable."

"Yes father, I've given him hot water to bath. Dinner will be served early to welcome our guest." Her father nods.

Kerhi call out invitation to all adults in his neighbourhood to join him in giving Erin a rousing reception. He waits a while for them to come into his compound before presenting drinks, kola nuts and some gold coins to his guest. Each invitee supports the presentation with some amount of cowries and gold coins. Erin is grateful for the kind gestures and takes the token.

It is the fifth day since he began to live amongst the earthlings. Some people talk about the stranger that has come to live in the same compound with a new widow.

They whisper any time Oma pass by. The maidens always pass by Oma's house on their way to the streams and market place in order to get a glimpse of Erin. They walk with measured steps and pro-actively wriggle their waists to catch his eyes.

Erin goes to the farm with Kerhi. He unsheathes his cutlass and they clear bushes for planting season. Kerhi gets tired and exercises his limbs. Seeing this, Erin persuades him to go home and take a rest.

"I can handle the remaining work."

"You will not be able to, but I'll go home to take some medicine and sleep for a while. Do the best you can and tomorrow we shall continue and burn the grasses."

Erin nods. Kerhi leaves. Erin uses fire from his eyes to burn the bushes to the point the ground is unblemished. He lingers in the farm until dusk and goes home.

In the morning, Erin wants to accompany Kerhi to the farm, but the old man insists he stays back and rest. Kerhi says he has been to the farm before dawn and seen the excellent work Erin did.

"I am very impressed with the work you did on the farm. You must be a great farmer. Your village must be missing you in this coming planting season."

Erin talks slowly, "He is very pleased indeed. He does not know I ravaged the farm with my fire within minutes." Kerhi smiles at him. "Of course he does not know," Erin smiles.

Kerhi tells him to rest. He picks up some little bags and heads to the farm. Erin waves him goodbye and goes into his hut.

Erin awakens from his siesta and comes to meet Oma in the kitchen. She is peeling some tubers of yam to cook yam porridge. The kitchen is made of bamboo sticks, mud, the roof is detachable giving to amount of light, and air the cook needs to get in.

"Can I help you with the cooking?"

Oma looks askew. "The kitchen is no place for a man. You should rather have gone to the farm with my father; he needs your hands there."

"I need to be here. If possible, I need to be around you at all times. My duty is to protect you."

"What do you mean?"

"Sorry, I meant that I can do all duties, I mean I can protect you."

"Protect me from what, the kitchen? A man needs more protection around the cooking area than the woman."

Erin causes the pot of boiling water to topple from the fire. He moves her away from it before the water or pot got to her. She is shocked. He did that because he must have sounded stupid to her.

"You see; now you see why fate had me stay around to save you. I'm here to protect you."

"Thank you, you saved me."

"I hope you weren't hurt. You are welcome. I will help you fix the fire and fetch some water." Oma thanks Erin and sit on the nearest kitchen stool to regain composure.

Chapter Ten

Keme does not respond to the greetings of three teenage boys who bow to him. They look at one another, shrug their shoulders and chatter as they walk on. Keme rushes into Kerhi's compound. He shouts, "Kerhi, Kerhi, Kerhi come out here."

"Who bellows my name like I've emptied his plantation of all his crops?" Kerhi comes out of the hut. "Oh, Keme, it is you, what brings you to my threshold at this hour, shouting loud enough to bring down my roof. I hope all is well with you and yours?"

Keme scratches his abdomen and position hands on his waist, "Where is your worthless daughter? Call her out."

"Whose daughter is worthless?" Kerhi looks about his compound.

Keme points at Oma's hut, "Oma, which other daughter do you have?"

"Keme, what brings you to my house?"

"You dare to accommodate a virile young man in your home, with your daughter still in mourning? Kerhi, that is very stupid of you."

"It is my home and I have every right to accommodate who I want and yes, my widowed daughter has gained wisdom of self-respect and family honour. She knows there is great difference between repute and disgrace. Also, guard your tongue. Mind the words you speak to me."

Keme spits on the ground, "She is a cheap harlot."

"Hold your foul tongue, hold it down Keme, and stuck it down your throat before it ignites my fury and I cut it off. If you intend to be aspersive over my daughter's character in my presence, then the gods forgive my actions, you shall cease to breath. I thank the gods your clan sent her packing. It would be vile fate had she remained in your family with you as her inheritor. You can devour your cousin's properties, my precious daughter will not contend with you. She will not share any ties with your accursed kindred. I'll send my kinsmen with her dowry by tomorrow."

"I dare you, I dare you Kerhi, let me see where you will get the huge amount of gold Omena used in buying her. You want to return the dowry so that she can delve into express bedding of different men, right. Of course, I am right. Smart one Keme, smart one. Oh, Kerhi, you have no character too, bringing a stranger under your roof with your daughter in residence," he hangs an opened palm, "Do you want to bet, any peasant can lay with her. You are a disreputable father of a harlot."

"I warn you Keme, don't you dare!"

"I don't need to say it, the people of Igowe know Oma has loose thighs and her private chamber must be deep and a public free flow as Igowe's largest sea."

"Keme," Kerhi run into his hut and comes out with a machete. He is about to strike at Keme.

Erin arrives and holds the cutlass. The blunt cutlass slightly cut him. His hand drips of blood. Kerhi let go of the cutlass and it clatters to the ground. Kerhi regrets he did not kill Keme and for hurting Erin.

Keme assesses Erin with scorn, "So you are the handsome devil that has come to possess my late cousin's wife. Barely few months have passed and she is still mourning for decency sake. Are you so shameless you had to come and do it under her father's roof?"

Erin's eyes are becoming red. When he speaks, his voice is cool. "I suggest you leave from here before your presence invokes more havoc."

"No, it is you that should leave from here; your intentions must be dishonourable. Go before you do more damage to my in-law's reputation."

"Keme Otukpo Adedhe Ovake. You derelict fool." Erin shouts Keme's full name.

Keme falls on the ground. He is shocked of the stranger's deep knowledge of his full name. No one else, except him, his father and grandfather knows this, and his father has only addressed him with the name this morning, when he had tried warning him of going to Oma's household to cause unneeded troubles. He does not waste a second when Erin ask him to get out a second time. He runs out as if a ghost is chasing him.

Oma returns from the stream with a pot of water on her head. She sees her father has bloodied hands. She throws the pot on the ground, the pot shatters into fat pieces.

"Father, what has happened?" She takes his bloodstained hands, "Are you hurt? What happened here? Who did this? Talk to me father." She begins to cry.

"I am fine, Oma." He pats her shoulder. "Erin is badly hurt from my machete. Please see to his wound."

"What, Erin is with wound? Father, what made you cut him?" Oma turns to Erin and examine his hand. She rushes to the backyard. She returns from the bush with some stems and leaves, she quickly pounds the plants in a mortar and makes an herbal mixture for his wound.

She stands in front of Erin. Her chest is heaving as she pants frantically. "Spread your hand." She instructs him. "Stretch it way forward and wide."

"Oma, at least, allow him sit." Kerhi drags a chair to where Erin is standing, and gently lowers him to sit. Oma kneels in front of him and applies the mixture on his blood stained hand. It helps stop the flow of blood.

"Thank the gods the cutlass was blunt, it didn't cut your hand deeply." Oma says.

Erin smiles and absent-mindedly stares at his hand. As she treats him, she sees no reaction from Erin. His face is expressionless as he thought of ways to avenge Keme.

The burning herbs that would have elicited great whine from Igowe's strongest warrior do not have any effect on Erin. Oma wonders. "It seems you are immune to pain." Oma's word jostles him from his thought. "You are not affected by the mixture. This is supposed to be painful, very painful."

Erin yowls and withdraws his hand. "I'm in so much pain. Please do it gently; to massage my hand with such vigour might break my bones. Oh, it hurts so much." Erin closes his eyes. The eyelids are fluttering open.

"Is that so," Oma raises an eyebrow.

He opens his eyes. "Hum, my ability to absorb pain is strong. I shall feel the pains later. My mother said I did bear pains a lot. Besides, this is not close to the wounds I have borne in the past."

Oma nods. She wraps his hand with a white cloth; afterwards she massages the hand with hot water. Kerhi brings a bottle of wine. Erin refuses to take it. He admonishes Erin to take few swallows.

Erin takes a sip and shakes his head. The strong brew tastes like water in his mouth.

"The strong brew will calm your nerves. It has a great healing effect." Kerhi says.

Erin nods and smiles. He holds his stomach because he has to feign he is feeling the effect of the drink. Kerhi smiles and goes into the kitchen with the cup.

Erin becomes sober. He reminds himself of his mission. He has almost forgotten his mission until Keme showed up today. Oma excuses herself to put away the calabash.

Erin says aloud, "that coward and unrepentant abominable murderer must feel my wrath. His path will be in the lake that burns with thunder and brimstone, which will be the ruination of him. The deities shall not have such immoral persons in the midst of good loving people; he will kill and kill. His thirst for blood is unsatisfactory. I shall not allow Keme and his dark sorcerers to persistently hound down my loyal subjects, their praises of me, and hope in my power of striking evil to the glory of justice, shall not be in vain." Fire stem from his eyes.

Oma returns with a bottle, Erin quickly douse the fire in his eyes. He is pleased to see the way Oma is smiling as she unties the bandage and applies ointment on the hand. He nods at her job well done. Erin thanks her as she covers the wound with a fresh bandage.

Chapter Eleven

Oma silently comes into Erin's room. The lamp burns low. He lay flat on the bed, fast asleep. She squats at the bedside and looks at his palms. There is no wound. Oma touch the hand to be sure and Erin jostles awake.

Erin clears his throat. "What are you doing here?"

Oma stands up and points a shaky finger at his hand. "I knew it. I have always suspected you are extraordinary. You do not feel pains. You're no mortal."

"I'm the god of thunder, and the rule thumb of vengeance. Your cries have brought me to earth. Oma called, my heart was cooed by her urgent summons."

"May the ancestors forbid I inconvenience the deities in such a manner? Who are you?"

"I'm Erin, the bolts of thunder are in my fingertips, and vengeance is always weighty in my heart. I have come to Igowe, into your life to avenge the evils Keme has done unto you. In due time, he shall pay for all his atrocities."

"If you are who you claim to be, you'll have to prove it. Why is your fury slow? Why have you not made Keme pay for his sins? You say my cry has brought you here, yet you sit and watch my heart pained as I continue to cry and wish the gods punished Keme. Why?"

Erin sits, "Because I've fallen in love with you, you bring embers different from the fire in my soul and my heart burn for more of it. I bid my time; so long, I attain my revenge, I will be gone from the earth. My vengeance lingers, because I've fallen in love with you, I don't want to leave so soon."

Oma angrily walks around the room, "I made no lover's call. I sought justice for my husband and children."

"I know but your love struck me. This feelings I've for you, is a pure affliction."

"What kind of a selfish god are you?"

Erin winces. He walks out of the room and goes out of the compound. Oma follows him with balled fists.

She drags his arm, "tell me the kind of god you are."

"I'm a god, who is irredeemably smitten with your love. I am not selfish."

"To hell with your love all I need from you oh, god is vengeance!"

Thunder begins clapping and the earth rotates. The earth becomes sloppy and Oma falls to the ground. Lightening covers the sky in silver and green veins. She shudders at the sight and calls onto Erin to save her. Erin is mad with rage, his broken heart call forth, violent thunderbolts from the sky.

Oma pleads and stretches her hands. Erin ignores her. He raises his hands and wills the wind and thunder strikes to subside. The earth suddenly comes to a standstill and Oma gasp for breath while the fury burns out of his eyes.

Erin speaks as he walks. "Vengeance is my state of mind. Love is the thought of a weakling." He shrugs his shoulders and runs off.

Oma looks bewildered at his angry figure. A voice whispers to her. "The gods are not perfect. Erin could not help the spiritual attraction to a physical. He has fallen in love with Oma. Because of his love for Oma, Erin came to do the vengeance himself. A love he denied in his heart. He took the body of a man; he came in the mind of a mortal and journeyed to Igowe with powerful vengeance in his soul and now, love blossoms in his heart. Oh, love oh love; a god is in love with a human."

"Who is that?" She turns around, looking for the owner of the voice. She screams, "I do not want love from a god. I only need vengeance for my husband and children."

The goddess of fertility comes to Edion, she curtsey, "My Lord Eternal, do you see that Erin has grown fonder of the widow. I fear earth will absorb him and he will dwell forever with the mortals. The spiritual world will have no place in his heart. I worry about my daughter. What will become of their betrothal? You know her anger can cause unending wind that can rumble the kingdom."

Edion plays with the golden ball, "Do not convey the imaginable to light. I already see calamity shaking our kingdom, if that ever happens;

we all will get so busy trying to fix the commotion. We may have to work for centuries to avert and contain the woes Erin's defaults will bring upon the kingdom."

"Great woes will befall the kingdom, and our sanctuary will know unrest."

"I know. Curtail your misgivings. Go goddess of fertility, go and attend to the women of Igowe that calls upon your name, seeking fruits of the womb. Go, go and bless them, put smiles upon their unhappy womb and plant great pride in their husbands' minds."

"My Lord eternal, I'm more worried about the union of our children. If my daughter does not wed with Erin, the god of her choice, in her anger, she may be unwilling to bless the barren women with fruitfulness. She can be that selfish."

"Enough, we shall be prepared for any consequences. If the inevitable happens, the women of Igowe will have no cry of babies in their huts for centuries, until when another will take over your daughter's realm, which is the least that can happen. That is the worst that can happen. Now go goddess of fertility, it is time for me to receive the sacrifices of Igowe, they have come to pay homage and give thanks for a successful season and aversion of earthquake." Edion laughs, "Erin's stampede caused an earthquake. He is causing the people sleepless night. The people are coming for a joyful thanksgiving."

"I pray their joy last long." She leaves.

Erin stops running. He senses Keme's presence on Oma's portion of the farm. He embarks on his mission to destroy him. He thinks a god must never break his oath of duty. Oma must think he is a foolish god. He is comforted with the earth that he is now bound to redeem his glory as a deity.

As he begins to run again, tears well up in his eyes. He stops and cautions himself that a god may hurt, but tears should never fall from his eyes. Worse is that his tears will cause a flood.

Erin groans, “I didn’t know I would suffer this much. Grace has not found me in love.” He lifts up his face to the sky.

The goddess of hope appears. He covers his chest when he sees her. She laughs and quickly enters through an uncovered patch on his chest.

“I hope you have brought a glimmer of hope to me.” Erin asks her.

“Good shall come out of your relationship with Oma, but the damages surpasses the short pleasures you would feel. The sin of this earth is extreme. It will bring greater harm than good to you. You should ascend to heaven if vengeance does not behold you. It is safer.”

“Oma cried to me. I will not leave until I dry those tears. I am close to my goal.”

“You will not reach your goal too soon. In trying, you might destroy Keme at the detriment of your throne above, is that how you will exert your vengeance? You will tarnish the duty towards the throne.”

“Get away from me; I need to carry out revenge on Keme.”

“Then keep calm, your rage is on the loose and it might consume everybody in Igowe. Will you destroy the just with the impious? Under such temperament, a bolt meant for one can take over a hundred. Keep calm, Erin. Your anger will not spare ninety-nine that are within range. Bear in mind, your anger is extremely savage. This is unlike you Erin. You judge all the earth, it wouldn't calm your anger and you will regret this unfair deed."

"I shall not raze the entire place because of one man. I am in my right frame of mind. If I find a second soul caught within the thunder, I shall clothe him or her with the spell of Vavo; it will keep the person safe."

"Abandon this vengeance for another day."

"I beg you, leave off my mind, and turn aside so that I can accomplish my mission. Once I am done, I will avail myself off this earth, I do not wish to remain here any longer. Hasten your thoughts out of my mind." Erin wills the spirit to be gone as he blows her into the air, and still she abides in him. "I shall not judge any other with my anger, Keme is my bane, and I shall make him the feast of my wrath. Be gone from here, I beg you do not lodge in my heart while I'm at this." He enters the farm and conjures mist to surround the land.

But the goddess continues to appeal. "Do not act violently against the lot. You have entered the farms, yet your nostrils flare in anger."

"I shall not strike those who are outside of this evil."

"I see your heart differently."

"Rise up and depart from my heart. Keme will destroy this village; if he does not, then the wickedness he sows in the people's life will destroy this nation. It is almost dawn; my will compels me to be done with him. Arise and flee from my mind, I do not seek your counsel. Lest you also perish amid the lightening of my wrath, vengeance is in the heart. Karma has spared him. I pledge, he shall not live a day more on earth. Or else a misfortune takes over me and I perish in this world."

Erin run and does not look back as he scans the entire region ahead. Morning dews begin to fall. Claps of thunder begin to applaud his vitality, he overturns the earth with his feet, flying and walking.

He sprints across the leaves, breaking plants and crops in his anger. But calmly he reviews the rules of vengeance, and slows his pace. In this state, his revenge may affect others if it is too temperamental. He becomes solemn for the safety of the unknown. The light from his eyes shine into the wide expanse of land in search of Keme and he spots him on one of his evil acts.

He sees Keme dropping threads into shallow holes. If Oma steps on any of the spot, she will run mad. Keme calls out Oma's name three times before he pours some red-hot liquid into the hole. This angers Erin. He stretches his hands and magically lifts Keme and flings him against a tree trunk. Erin did not let him recover from the fall. He run towards him and pumps bolts of thunder into Keme until he swell and float on electrifying waves.

Oma has been running after Erin. She comes in view before he injects the final bolts into Keme. She screams his name aloud for him to stop. "No, Erin…Stop. I can now see you are a god."

"Let me do this. I do not want to leave in cold defeat, let me release this rage in me. My spirit boils for vengeance."

"No," Oma boldly put down his hands and the hex disappears from Erin's fingertips.

"Why did you stop me? I boiled to exert my vengeance and leave off your world and you stopped me at the peak."

"Something came over me. I do not know what it was." She looks downcast.

"It was foolishness." Erin walks away, seething in anger.

Oma looks at Keme who is chickening on the ground. "I should have just let him kill you, but that would have been too fast, I want you to suffer, I want you to die slowly, I want you to pay for every evil deed you've committed against me. I want doom to spell every letter of your name." She stamps her foot on his stomach repeatedly and Keme coughs out blood.

The goddess of fertility sits with her daughter. "Stop sulking. I spoke to the Lord Eternal, and he assured me that your marriage with Erin will hold."

"And about Erin, how are we sure he will honour this union. Mother, our Lord Eternal do not have reigns over his son's personal decision. You know as well as I do, that Erin's decision does not sway."

"Your engagement was ordained long before you and Erin were born. He cannot bring disgrace to this kingdom. Edion will not condone it." Damena stands and flaps her flowing gown with force. "Damena, be rest assured Erin will make you his wife."

"Edion could not stop his descent to earth. What makes you feel he can make him ascend heaven if Erin decides to stay amongst the earthlings?"

"He will be back. My pretty daughter, worry less."

"I hope so, mother. I really hope that woman does not get in the way of my love, or else I will not spare her."

"Erin will be back. Come, sit with your mother." Damena haughtily returns to the seat. Her mother combs her hair with a golden brush and gives her a head massage.

"Damena, I want to tell you something."

"Yes mother, speak, I am listening."

"The deity of sun is very handsome and prosperous with his powers."

Damena quickly turns to face her mother. "I will marry no one else. I will wait for the one I am betrothed. Give me more of this massage. Mother, it is so soothing." The goddess of fertility adds ointment to her palm and gently massages her daughter's head.

Chapter Twelve

Erin creates a distance between himself and Oma. Any time Oma comes into his presence, Erin makes excuses for her to either leave or he goes out. They barely talk to each other. They are compelled to converse whenever Kerhi is in their midst. Erin feeds from the farm during work hours; Oma only pretends to bring an empty plate to his hut for her father not to suspect their grievances for one another.

Erin seeks Kerhi's permission to build a hut in the farmland for a temporal stay. Kerhi readily agrees. Kerhi and Oma join him to cut down trees and dig mud. In Kerhi's presence, Erin has no choice but to eat the meal Oma serve for him. He accepts the plate with a curt nod and eats, she smiles and dishes food for her father. She watches as Erin finish his meal, drinks some water and belch. After they leave, it takes seconds for Erin to erect the hut and seals it with invisible lightening.

To find out about Erin's depth of knowledge, Keme goes to see the witches of Apele. Keme flies in a winnowing basket to get to the coven. The way he marches into the dark monstrous cave, shows he is frequent to the place.

Many horrid statues line the hallway, golden snakes' swim on the floor while black snakes mate one another. Keme sidestep the coiled reptiles and push open the great double doors. The room instantly light up with green flames, smoke comes out from a pot of boiling water.

Keme puts his hands at the back of his waist and bows to the witches. The wild witch-leader of the coven smiles and reveals diamond teeth. The horrid scars on her face did not compliment the beauty of the gems. The sparkles from the diamond mirror her fellow witches' bodies wrapped in black fur wrappers and red choking beads.

She curls her long fingers, "Keme, you visit us again. I hope you loved the way those poisons worked for you."

"Yes, oh, great witch. It was powerful and my mission accomplished. However, there is a problem, which is why I am back here. I need you to do me a favour."

"What do you want?"

"I want to be made a monster."

She laughs sinisterly. "Interesting, I thought wickedness was only found among witches of Apele. Here is an evil wizard in our midst." The other witches laugh.

Their mockery irritates Keme. He smiles, "aha, interesting. I see you witches have had nothing to laugh about for a long time." He sneers.

"I would hire a better jester. Your soul is too dark for humour." She smiles broadly. "Wait here, our initiation is about to begin. I will be with you shortly." She sensuously traces the lines on his lips with a finger. Keme bobs and swallow spittle.

A full moon appears, a wolf howls and the rituals begin. The inner circle of witches assembles to initiate new members. Each member takes an oath of loyalty after drinking blood from a black coal pot and eaten flesh of vultures. They rove over the coven with brooms and hum shrieking chants of worship.

Most of the new converts are elderly widowed women who have been humiliated, beaten, stripped off their family ties and rights, ostracised from their communities, and banished to the evil forest for wild beasts to feed on them. The wild witch found them before the beasts and brought them at different times to the coven.

The witches fly down. Music plays. They begin to dance and sweep the coven with their brooms. The wild witch gestures Keme to follow her. He follows her to the throne.

She sits, “Kneel,” she says and eats a black apple. Keme looks around, “you, I said, kneel.”

“Me,” he taps his shoulder.

“Yes you, kneel,” Keme grudgingly bends on one knee, “no, the two knees.”

“As you wish,” Keme kneels.

“Good, now hold your head high and crawl towards me.”

Keme quickly stands and dust his kneecaps, “what, why should I crawl towards you? Do you realise you are talking to a proud warrior of Igowe? I will not do that. Who are you anyway?”

“I am Cocovkpe, the wild witch of Apele. A chicken warrior of Igowe has once again come to seek for my help and he shall do whatever I ask him to do. Kneel, hold your head high and look me in the eyes as you crawl towards me."

Keme does as she says. He stops at the foot of her throne. She throws the apple seeds at him. Keme angrily looks at her. She let out a shrieking laugh and stands. She caresses his body and grabs his manhood. Keme gasps and his eyes widen. She bends and whispers on his lips. He clenches his jaw in anger.

Erin and Kerhi go fishing at night. At the river, they are trying to hoist a big catfish when Oko-siamese fish leads a school of fish, shoal of snake and other aquatic inhabitants in a processional music exercise through a stream lane. Oko sights them and command the procession to advance in their direction.

They let go of the fish, put off the lamp and run to the nearest tree. Kerhi gestures for Erin to beat his cutlass on the tree. Erin nods and quickly extracts his cutlass. Together they smack their cutlasses on the tree. It is a loud ovation to distract the procession from heading towards them. The aquatic inhabitants begin to dance to the rhythm of their cutlasses. They energetically twist and jump to the beats. They exhaust their energy and go back into the water.

Kerhi puts a hand on his chest. “That was very close.”

“What was that about?”

“Erin, I am glad you followed my moves. Your beats were better than mine were. Have you done that before?”

Erin shakes his head. “I do not even know what that was about.”

“That was Oko and her crusade. They do not like the fishermen that come to catch creatures of the water. They can unexpectedly come upon the farmer and eat his or her feet. Playing the tree song is a way to distract them."

Erin sheaths his cutlass. "So why did you risk us coming out?"

"I could risk fishing at this hour because I get rewarded with big fishes."

"Oh, I see. That was a narrow escape we had. You should be very careful then. You might not always be lucky."

"Yes, come on hurry. Let us leave. They may gather momentum and come back for us."

They pack their tools and hurry out of the stream. They pick race when they saw Oko and her procession coming out of the water again. They reach the farm and stop to catch their breath.

Erin sees Kerhi is breathing very fast. "Should I get you some water?"

"Yes, please." Kerhi coughs.

Erin enters his hut and comes back with an empty cup. "The water pot is empty. I did not remember to fill it yesterday."

"It is okay. Erin, I will manage until I get home." He hiccups, "Why don't you come back to the house. You are not taking care of yourself. There should always be water in the house."

"I know, I will fill the pot tomorrow," Erin takes Kerhi's arm. "You strain your muscles too much. Come, I will walk you home."

"Will you stay the night in the farm?"

"Yes, I will come back to my hut."

"Erin, why did you suddenly leave the warmth of our comfortable hut? What went wrong? Is it Oma or the villagers? Did you hear side talks that were displeasing to your ears? Do not take it to heart Erin, the people of Igowe can talk and talk that is where it ends because they are good-natured."

Erin shakes his head. He is sad that Kerhi does not know people like Keme exist.

"It is nothing of those sorts, really. I will be fine here."

"Erin, but there is no water, what will you do when you grow thirsty tonight."

"I will manage. Please do not worry about me. I will be fine. I should walk you halfway so that I do not grow thirsty. Let us go, Oma will be anxiously waiting for your return."

Kerhi smiles dreamily. "Oma, she gets unnecessarily worried at times. I wish she will remarry and have a man and children to give this care and attention." Erin smiles, they walk silently, each man to his thoughts.

In the morning, Oma comes to the farmhouse with a pot of water. She sees Erin trying to cook. He kneels to the level of the tripod to blow the fire with his mouth.

"No, not that way, it is dangerous to put your face close to the fire."

She carries the pot into the hut and quickly comes out with a basket of vegetables.

She resets the firewood and fans the fire with the basket lid. "My foolishness has caused you to make the kitchen your position." She faces him. "Erin, please forgive me, come back home."

Erin stares at her and he thinks aloud, 'she is truly sorry.'

She washes and slices the vegetables. Erin continues to fan the fire. She goes to pick some condiments from her farm. She sits on a stool and prepares the meal.

Oma tastes the soup and covers the pot, "The food is ready, I will be leaving." She stands.

"Stay, and eat with me."

"It is late, I do not want to go back home in the dark, I did not come with a torch."

"Erin is here, I am a light in your path. I will walk you through any dark path and shadow. I will safely walk you home, even on the darkest night. Have no fear."

Oma nods and sits. She dishes the food and they eat silently. "The moon has appeared, it is very bright and will light my way home." She put the plates together. "I am going home."

"Wait," Erin takes the dishes into the house and returns with a shawl. He wraps it around her shoulders.

She smiles and snuggles the shawl around her body. "Thank you,

Erin."

"Let us go," Erin walks away.

She walks behind him, admiring his broad back. "Oma, oh, be decent." She chastises herself for shamelessly glaring lustfully at another man.

As they make their way through some bushy paths, Keme appears to be trailing them. He watches them and menacingly tweaks his moustache. "I thought I only accused Oma falsely. She has found her way into another man's arms so soon. She did not take time to mourn the man she claimed to love so much. Oh, poor Omena, he must be wreathing in his grave. His wife is so shameless," he spits on the ground.

When they go far off, Keme turns around and run to Erin's house. He ransacks through Erin's possessions and finds nothing spectacular. "Nothing, I cannot find any clue of who he is." He puts hands on his waist and puffs. "This is strange. There is definitely something extraordinary about him, I just have to place my hands on what it is."

Oma stops walking. She touches her wrist. "Erin, I think I must have dropped my bracelet."

"Oma, are you sure?"

"Yes, I felt this emptiness just now. I touched my wrist and realised it is gone."

"I will bring it to the house tomorrow morning. I am sure it is lying somewhere in the kitchen."

"No, let us go back and look for it."

"That will make you late; it is a delay, an unnecessary delay. I have said I will bring it to the house in the morning."

"No Erin, it is the most precious jewel my husband gave me, I have never slept without it ever since that night."

"What night do you mean?"

Oma does not say anything and quickly walk in the direction of the farm. Erin sighs and follows her.

Keme hears footsteps. He has been rummaging Erin's room. He is about to open a golden pot when he hears Oma and Erin's voices.

"I hope we find it." Oma says.

"Check in the kitchen while I look around the fireplace." Erin says.

"It seems they did not get enough of each other." Keme says under his breath. He peeps at Oma maliciously. He begins to run and kicks a pot. He carries the pot and leaves through the window.

He gets tired of running. Keme sits at the foot of a giant tree. He smiles sheepishly, rubs his palms, and opens the pot. Vapours of flames pops all over his face. Keme screams and throw the cover away. The pot and its cover disappear into the sky. Blackness covers his face, only his lips is still pink. He scrambles and run away, falling and getting up in fear.

Oma sees the bracelet in his hut. She joyfully picks it up from the floor and wears it. She shakes her head and walks out, "Erin, I found it."

She rams her foot into a broom, “Oh, oh, my foot. Oh, it hurts.”

He runs to her, “Sorry, Oma.” He holds her shoulder and guides her to the stool.

“Erin, I hurt my foot, and it hurt so badly.” Erin kneels. He puts her foot on his thigh to examine the wound.

A sharp stick has protruded her flesh. He tries to pull it out but Oma’s incessant wailing prevents him. He gestures for Oma to look behind. “I think your father has come to look for you.” Oma turns around. He immediately raises her thigh and jerks the stick out of her foot. She screams and beats his shoulders with her hands. “It is done. You will cry out the pain then feel better, trust me.”

Oma thrashes her foot. “It hurts so much.” Tears gather in her eyes.

Erin could not bear to see those tears, “If you will permit me.”

“What,” Oma stares at his chest.

Erin raises her leg and places her foot on his chest. Oma feels a burning sensation build up in her body. It seems Erin is injecting something mysteriously calm with physical and spiritual effect; she inhales, allowing the heat from his body move immaculately into her body. Oma closes her eyes to absorb the healing effect.

Erin admires Oma, *‘her beauty is flawless. She does not look like what she has been. The pains and sorrow seems stashed in another’s body and soul. One part of me wants to deal with Keme and return to the upper world as soon as possible, while the other just wants to linger on and stay under the moon with Oma.’* He thought. “Oma,” he taps her

knee.

Oma exhales deeply. "Hmmm…I feel good, so much better." She checks her foot and is shocked. "The wound is gone. There is no trace of a scar." Oma quickly gets up, "I should go. Father must be worried. I have never stayed out this late."

"Are you sure, what about that night? Oma, what happened on that night?" Oma is shy. "You cannot tell me. Anyway, you cannot possibly go home. The moon has disappeared; there will be a heavy downpour soon."

Oma creases her brow and wonders what are father might be thinking.

"Did you tell your father your destination?"

"Yes," she says quickly. It is a lie. Her father was not at home when she left. He had told her Erin did not have water so she had thought it wise to bring him a pot of water.

"Okay, good, when the rain begins, he will understand why you could not come home. He will relax knowing you are in safe hands."

Oma stares at his muscular arms and wishes she could caress it. She stands at once and misses a step. Erin gets hold of her before she hit the ground. Their faces are inches close. They gaze into one another's eyes for some minutes. Oma is enamoured with Erin's looks. He clears his throat. She straightens her body. He takes her into the house and puts her on the bed.

"I will be outside." Oma wants to say something but shuts her mouth.

Erin gives a curt nod and leaves.

He goes to the pond and folds his arms. The night breeze lures a stale fragrance to his nose. He traces the odour to its spot. Erin finds a young dinosaur crying by its mother. The animal looks up, and Erin marvels at its enthralling eyes. Their eyeballs stay locked together for some minutes.

Erin moves the baby dinosaur from its mother's side. He digs a grave and buries the sticky mammal. He takes the little dinosaur to the farmhouse. He feeds it and leaves it in the warmth of the kitchen.

He prays for morning to come fast. Rain begins to fall. Erin goes into the house. He puts some shawls on the floor and lies on the bedding. He listens to the rain pelting the roof for a while and falls asleep.

Chapter Fourteen

Erin wakes to the sound of chirping birds. “Oma,” he is startled when he did not hear her response. Erin gets up and goes outside. The surrounding is neat. He checks the kitchen and backyard. She is not around the farmhouse. He scratches his chin.

Erin makes a dash to Kerhi’s compound, there he finds Oma. She is sweeping the compound while she sings. She raises her head up and smiles. “Erin, you are here.”

He brushes his hair with his hands, “Her smile is like the radiant morning sun. This should be the first sun that should set on me, every day,” Erin says softly. He walks towards her.

“Erin, you are here. I am sorry I left without informing you. You were sleeping so peacefully, I did not want to disturb you.”

“That is okay, you should have woken me. How is your father?”

“He is sleeping.”

“He is sleeping at this time of the day? That is unusual of him. I hope he is well?”

“Yes, he is fine. It is just a little fatigue from yesterday’s labour. He will be stronger when he wakes up. His herbal tea is brewing. Do you want some?" Oma drops the broom and heads to the kitchen.

"No, thank you. I just wanted to know if you are doing well. I will leave now. Please extend my regards to your father. I shall wait for him at the farm." Erin nods and goes away.

Oma continues sweeping and singing beautifully. Ola walks into the compound. She goes behind Oma and closes her hands over her eyes.

"Ola, I know it is you so come out of your pranks."

Ola rounds on Oma, "you can easily tell it is me."

"Have you forgotten we wear the same perfume?"

"Yes, we share the same fragrance," Ola takes a small bottle from between her cleavages. "Here please, you will pour some of the perfume into my bottle. I will give it back when I buy mine on the forthcoming market day."

"Do not worry. I have several bottles in the house. I will give you two bottles."

Ola jumps excitedly and hugs her. "Oma, you are a gem. You are as pleasant as the lavender perfume. I want to smell nice on the day you introduce me to Erin."

"Really, this morning would have been a great opportunity. Erin was here a while ago."

Ola looks around, "thank the gods I did not meet him. My hair is not properly dressed, my face is not scrubbed and made up and I am not even wearing perfume." She sprays the little in the bottle on her nape and armpits. "I am not even feeling fresh."

Oma laughs, "Ola, Ola your natural body smells fresher than these fragrances. Either by day or night, you can face any of your admirers."

Ola's face beams. She takes another broom, ties her wrapper firmly and joins her friend in sweeping.

Kerhi comes out of his hut. He ties his wrapper securely and brushes his teeth with a long chewing stick.

"Greetings Pa Kerhi," Ola says and curtseys.

"My dear, you are welcome," Oma brings water in a bowl. Kerhi rinses his mouth with some water, squishes and spit the water.

"Greetings father," Oma takes the cup.

"Oma, my beautiful child, well done, I did not see you before retiring to bed last night."

"Father, I went to bed early."

"But you were not in your room."

"Father, maybe I had gone to attend nature's call when you checked in on me."

Kerhi nods and takes his seat. He applies balm on his ankles and wrist. He sniffs a pinch of herbal powder medicine. Ola takes her broom to the kitchen.

"Father, Erin was here. He said he would wait at the farm."

"That is strange; I usually meet him up at the farm, I wonder why he did not send words but chose to come all the way. I should go at once to the farm; it might be an urgent matter brought him here."

Oma fiddles with the broom head, "No, no father, it is nothing serious. I guess he was passing by, you woke up a little too late, so he was concerned."

"Yes, but it is still strange that Erin called so early. Where was he heading to or coming back from?"

She stutters, "Father, he is an adult, Erin is a grown man that now knows the map of Igowe, perhaps, he took a morning stroll."

"Well, I will not go to the farm today. Oma, you will run an errand for me. Check in the barn, there are some seedlings, tell him to plant as much as he can, I will join him in the evening. You can leave after my meal."

"Yes, father, I will."

"Oma, are you all right? You are sweating despite it is a very cool morning."

"I. Am…am fine father. I am fine, truly." she wipes the sweat on her forehead." Kerhi nods.

Ola is eavesdropping on their conversation from the kitchen. Oma enters the kitchen and set to prepare breakfast. Ola looks at Oma suspiciously.

Oma catches her questioning stare. "Ola, why are you staring at me in such a manner?" She dusts some salt off her fingertips and stands. She holds Ola's elbow. "Is anything the matter?"

"Hmmm…I saw the way you fidgeted when your father was questioning you about your whereabouts and Erin's visit. Oma, I could see how frightened you were. You told a lie, Oma you were telling lies. Your father might be too old to sense these things, but I am not. Oma, where did you pass the night? Was it with Erin? You slept in his house, am I right? Oma, you love him." Oma turns away from her. Ola takes her hand and swirls Oma to face her, "answer me Oma, are you having an affair with Erin."

Oma takes Ola's hand and put it on her chest, "Believe me Ola, I do not love him, and this is the first and last time I will clarify you on this. Yes, I did not sleep on my bed last night. I was with Erin in the farmhouse. I slept on the bed and he was on the floor the whole night." Ola opens her eyes and mouth in disbelieve. "Ola, it is not what you are thinking, you are imagining silly things. I was there to give him a message from father."

"Oma, you are lying again. Your father did not have the slightest clue of where you had gone. Did you not just tell him you had gone to use your chamber pot when he checked up on you? You are speaking with double tongues. I do not know what to believe any more." She inhales deeply.

"Stop talking nonsense."

"Oma, what are you hiding? You know I love Erin. What is it you are not telling me? You are not being sincere. I love Erin and you know that. The least you could do is to confide your emotions in me, and in turn I will reign in my feelings and set my cap on another."

"Ola, I promise you, Erin and I share no bond. I injured my foot while at his house. I would have come back home if I had not been caught up in the rain, so I had to stay back and returned before cock crow."

"So, Erin was your escort."

"No, I did not even wake him before leaving, which was why he came to check if I was here."

Ola looks at Oma more suspiciously. "You said you hurt your foot. Show me the injury."

Oma is about to bear her foot when she recalls Erin has completely healed the wound with magic. She drops her leg and smiles wearily, "the wound is an ugly sight. You might throw up if you see it."

Ola snaps her fingers towards Oma's foot, "I insist. I want to see it. Raise it," she does an up and down motion with her hand, "raise the foot up, Oma."

Oma looks embarrassed. "Never mind, Ola, it was just a small cut. It was nothing serious."

"Oma, I do not believe this." Ola says and storms out of the kitchen. Kerhi hides at the side of the kitchen and prays Ola does not turn back. She stands for a moment and leaves the compound.

He has been listening to their conversation. His brows narrow confusingly. He thinks Oma is sincere with her friend to an extent, but he wonders why Oma has lied to him. He shakes his head and stealthily returns to his seat.

After a while, Oma brings his meal. She curtseys after placing a cup of water by the side. Kerhi washes his hand. "Oma, after my meal, I will head to the farm. You can carry on with your activities for the day."

"Okay father, if you say so. I will get your medicine bag and tools ready."

Oma goes into her father's hut. Kerhi eats in deep thought. He drinks his medicine and rests his back.

Erin reaches the farm and goes to the kitchen. The dinosaur is gone. He goes to its mother's graveside, but he is lost on which site he had buried her. There is no trace of the fresh grave. He stamps his foot. "This is the very spot I buried the dead dinosaur. Has the rain washed off her grave?" Erin looks about him convincingly.

The god of mystery appears, "Erin, that animal was created to trail you. It has taken your fingerprint to the coven of Apele. Your hands were marked for proper identification by her body. The baby dinosaur, it followed you home to access your personal surrounding and gather more information. It is on its way back to give the witches feedback." The god of mystery disappears.

Erin is now convinced of what happened when his hands were sticky to the dead mammal's body.

An apparition appears. It is a reflection of Erin. He says, "Your task should be accomplished soon. Erin, move fast on your duty that bound you to this earth. You must complete your task at once and leave the earth. A great storm gathers in the coven of Apele, you do not want to witness it. A great evil will rear to the surface of Igowe." The apparition fizzles.

The goddess of hope appears, "Erin, you do not have much time." She roams around him.

"Goddess of hope, you told me there would be blossoms of love between Oma and I. You gave me false hope. Dear fair goddess, you gave Erin false hope."

"It is not false. Only there is no time, your love is timeless and this period is odd and even."

"Tell me of the even, spare me the odds."

"Okay, I will tell you…"

"Erin," Kerhi calls out.

The goddess of hope disappears. Erin rush back to the farmhouse. He sees Kerhi coming out from the hut.

"I greet you." He nods.

Kerhi smiles warmly and pats his back. "I was looking for you. You were nowhere in sight. I hope all is well?"

"I am fine. I was just far off in the bush. I hope you are feeling much better. I was at the house earlier. Oma told me you would rest longer."

"Yes, I am stronger and healthier." Kerhi gently flexes his muscles. He gives a bag to him. Erin smiles and takes the bag. "I will wait for you to have breakfast, and then we can work on the farm."

Erin checks the content of the bag, "I will break my fast after work. Should I get you something to eat? Oma prepared a delicious meal last night." Erin looks at Kerhi, "I hope you were not angry she did not return home last night, the rain made it impossible."

"It is okay, I was only worried. Let us go to the farm." Kerhi grins. Erin nods and goes to take his cutlass from the kitchen.

They walk to the farm in silence. As the morning sun begins to set, they bury the last seeds in the soft soil and exercise their limbs. They return to Erin's house. He serves the soup from previous night and they eat together in a plate.

Kerhi clears his throat, "Erin, there might be a possibility, a slim chance that someone had seen you and Oma together. Perhaps, someone had a glimpse of Kerhi's daughter leaving the house of a man who is not her husband, at an ungodly hour." He clears his throat again and drinks some water. "I hope you know the implications of my words?"

"I do not get your points. Please, convey your words appropriately." Erin sips some water.

Kerhi looks at him sternly. Erin scratches his chin and sips more water. Kerhi's face softens. "My daughter is a young widow. An accusation that she is an adulterer is still hanging around her neck. She has been through many bad times," Kerhi shakes his head solemnly. "Erin, you are a virile handsome man, Oma is a beautiful matured woman. Both of you do not have to make excuses for your love. You do not need to sneak around in the dark. Come out to the light with your love."

Erin raises his hands in protest, "Hold on, Kerhi. Was that what you were insinuating? Oh, no Kerhi, you are mistaken. Truly, you are mistaken. Oma and I do not share an intimate bond."

"Hmmm, Oma denies the love she has for you as well. But, I am her father. Even the night she went from being a maiden to a woman, I knew it. She cannot hide anything from me. I see deep emotions in her eyes, and hear her heart beat fast whenever she mentions your name or someone else does. Erin, I see the same in your eyes and hear it in your voice. You have feelings for my daughter."

Erin lowers his gaze, "so that was what happened that night. I wonder if there will be a glimmer of hope for my love," he says softly. He cannot confess his love to Kerhi, the time for him to depart the earth is near, and it will be of no use. Erin is devastated. He wishes he could grab this opportunity to confess his love, but he is powerless in a world he did not belong.

"Kerhi, it is true I love your daughter. But I cannot express my emotions towards Oma. It is true I really love her but I cannot do any honourable process to woo her love forever. I am pained to dishonour your knowledge of my love for her. Please, forgive me." He stands.

"Have you bedded my daughter? She might not be chaste but she has virtues. Erin, did you lay with my daughter?" Erin looks at Kerhi in shock. "Answer the questions; did you lay with my Daughter?"

Erin flays his hands in anger, "No, we did not and never will."

"Then you must pack up and evacuate the farmhouse, you are no longer welcome here."

He nods, "Your hospitality has been kind, I will leave as soon as my work here is complete."

"What work, the planting season is over."

"The task is only privy to the gods." Erin leaves Kerhi in a confused state.

Kerhi regrets his hasty decision. "I love him to be around, but I fear for my daughter's peace of mind. It is best he leaves from our lives."

Chapter Fifteen

Cocovkpe is sated from Keme making love to her. She drags her nails across his chest and kisses his nipples.

When she bites hard on his nipple, Keme yells. "Oredia, you witch. What was that? You are so wild."

"That is why I am called the wild witch," She bites harder on the second nipple and Keme jerks in pain.

She gives him a bewitching smile. "That was for saying yes so late. I should have enjoyed you on that day you came with that request. You turned down my proposal, I am glad you have made the right decision."

Keme relaxes and smiles. He playfully mounts her body and she giggles. He is about to thrust when she pushes him off. He lands on the floor with a thud. He kneels and rubs his buttocks.

She creeps on him slowly. Keme falls flat on his back. She seduces him until his penis hardens. She whispers into his ears. "Hum, Keme is a sweet, sweet warrior in bed. I love your hefty sword. You wield it with much strength. It only lacks passion. I hope your manhood grows fonder in this covenant. You are as hard as a rock. I am a generous leader. My witches will suck out of this wondrous nectar," she kisses him soundly on the nose.

Keme's eyes widen and he tries to sit up. She pushes him back to the floor. "Oh, no…that was not part of the seal," he says. He sits up and ties his wrapper. He stands up but she holds him down with magic.

Ten witches fly into the room in an instant. They giggle and line up. Each witch takes turn on Keme. They make wild love to him. Keme looks on repulsively at their retreating figure.

Cocovkpe blows a kiss at him. She closes the door on him and there is a heavy click of the heavy bolt. Keme's limbs become free from the spell. He remains on the floor in exhaustion. He is very angry and bangs his fists on his laps.

Erin has been on prowl to find Keme, enquiries reveals Keme has not been around the village. He has little time to carry out his mission. The goddess of hope has not appeared to him since Kerhi's intrusion. He concludes there is no hope for Oma and him to have a love story.

To pass time, Erin works on the farm with Kerhi-watering the crops and cutting out weeds. They rarely speak to one another. Nods and body gesticulations transmits messages between them. They did not share a conversation beyond 'yes' and 'no'.

The goddess of fertility comes to Edion. She kneels before the mirror, "See how they have reduced the son of Edion to an ordinary farmer. Oh, that common peasant, he treats our Erin with arrogance. See how shabbily the human treats a god. He belittles our Erin."

Edion looks moody. "My Lord Eternal, did you hear what I have just said?"

Edion spins his golden ball, "This hostility is good for his course and our wishes. The cold shoulders of Kerhi will make him feel unwelcome. It will make him dispatch his duty faster than I thought. The warm reception was making him comfortable. Their warmth was explicitly hospitable. This new cold will bring him back home."

She smiles, "you are right. We will have him back very soon." She shakes her head, "If this wedding does not hold, I fear Damena will withhold her fertility blessings from the world."

"Don't bore me with her tantrums. Tell the god of host to prepare Erin and Damena' wedding banner. The god of host should make the first call of our children's forthcoming nuptial. I want the best arrangements. He should make the invitation in rainbow colour. Once Erin is home, we will conclude the wedlock of our precious god and goddess."

"This is good news; I am so relieved with this development. The heaven and earth are full of my favour. I shall share flowers so that the gods can perceive the fragrance of the royal banquet to come. My Lord Eternal, I am so happy." She touches her head on his feet three times. She bows happily and leaves.

She goes to the god of host and tells him the details of the wedding preparations. She carries a basket full of flowers on her way out. The goddess of fertility gives flowers to any gods and goddesses she meets on the way. They wonder what is making her so happy. She passes by the gate of purgatory. She steps backward and throws some flowers into the cell. Agbavwo walks forward; he holds the gate and grunts.

She hurries off to break the news to her daughter. Damena is excited, she takes her mother's hands and waltz, "Oh, mother, this news gladdens my heart, my soul is thrilled, and oh, my feet are so happy." She runs towards the mirror and admires her face and figure. Damena runs back and stands in front of her mother, "Oh, fairest of goddess you made this happen. This news gladdens my heart, my soul is thrilled, oh, my feet are so happy, come mother, dance with me." They sing beautifully and dance around. Damena's laughter rings across the kingdom.

Edion hears the sound of her laughter and he smiles satisfactorily. He grabs manna from the sky, pops it into his mouth, and chew thoughtfully. Erin checks the sprouting plants. He nods at Kerhi and leaves. Kerhi put his hand on his waist. He stares guiltily at Erin.

"What is wrong with me? Why do I have to be so hard on Erin?" He shakes his head, "No, he is an amazing young man. I need to foster peace between us. Even if he is not in love with my Oma, we can still have a cordial connexion." He spreads his palms, "he came like a seraph and makes me labour less. My hands are like a baby's soft faeces this season." He slings his hoe over his shoulder and picks up the cutlass. "The gods willing, I shall speak to him tomorrow." Kerhi heads out of the farm.

Edion's brows creases, "Oh, no Kerhi, do not speak of reconciliation, the gods are not willing. The gods are already looking forward to my Erin and Damena's wedding. But how will you know this? You are just a mere mortal, a human who uses a god like a peasant farmer."

"My Lord Eternal, he does not know Erin is a god. From what I can see, Erin is enjoying it eh. Who would not enjoy such a moor in the universe? Oma is a beautiful damsel; any man can do anything for her sake."

Edion bangs the ball on the armrest, a rabbit's head comes out of the golden ball, "ouch, what was that for? I am your Scribes and not a mere ball."

"Keep quiet and let me think," Edion slings the golden ball towards the golden mirror and repossess it into his palm before it hit the mirror. The rabbit pants and closes its eyes. "Oh, just look at my son; he shouldn't have had a dip in the river. Obviously, Igowe gives the skin a natural tan. I might not recognise my heir when he ascends the upper world. It is not yet time for the rainy season, but let me send some showers to cool the earth."

The rabbit quickly opens its eyes, "What are you saying? There has been rain…" Edion sends down rain.

Erin runs into the hut before a drop of rainwater touches him. Kerhi lifts his face to the cloud. He smiles that the rain has come. He walks on thinking that his and Erin's ceasefire shall be fruitful and cool.

Chapter Sixteen

Erin is lying on a bamboo stretcher bed and looks boringly at the sky. He conjures fire on his fingertips. He uses the flames to caress his arms. He bends his head over the stretcher's edge and sees her.

Oma bounds towards him with a bright smile. Her hips bounce as she sidesteps the plants. Erin stands and passionately stares at her. He admires the way her braids cups her face. A dark scowl clouds his face.

He does not expect to see her on the farm. They have not seen each other in five days and four nights. He suspects Kerhi has been doing all things possible so that they have no encounter. He wonders what brings her to the farmhouse. He sees some young men behind her and quickly quenches the fire. The men are discussing and wearing cocky grins and laughing aloud.

Oma comes to his side, "Erin, I have brought the village youths, they requested to see you. Father asked me to show them the way." Her eyes says '*I wanted to see you too, that is why I have brought them this far.*'

The youths reach the farmhouse. They call out greetings to Erin. They shake one another's hands.

"Erin, good to see Igowe is treating you nicely," says a youth.

"Yes, a fair weather, and fair friends. I am honoured," says Erin.

"We have come to invite you to join our age grade in preparation for the festival; it is in the next five days. We have four days for practice, and the morning of the event for our last rehearsal. Would you join us?" says Maduve.

"That is wonderful, but I am afraid, I will not be able to join you in practice."

Oma pouts, "Please Erin, it is fun and exciting. I am sure you have never seen anything like it, I promise you. You would love it."

With the way she sexily pouts her lips; Erin is tempted to agree with her. The youths look hopeful.

"I am sorry. I will not be joining the masquerade team, but I will surely attend the wonderful event," says Erin.

The young men smile. "Please Erin, we have one more request," Maduve says.

"What then?"

"We hope you can avail the farmhouse for our practice. We are the masquerades. The nearness of the pond is perfect; it is a great advantage for our performances' success."

"You can certainly practice here with permission from Oma's father. I am just a guest here; this land is not my home." Oma looks unhappy he said that. "If he says yes, then feel at home, the venue is yours."

She wriggles her hands, "Father has given his consent if you agree to their request."

Erin is ecstatic and claps his hands. "Then it is settled. You are all welcome. It will be an honour to watch the drama before the grand finale of its performance."

Oma claps her hands in glee. "Can I join you to watch them during practice?"

He could not refuse Oma. He needs her to be around him as much as possible. "Yes, with your father's permission."

"Father has already given his consent. He said I am safe with you."

"He said that? Did he really say you could be with me in the farmhouse," Oma gives him a questioning stare, "hum, eh, I mean did he really grant you permission to watch the practice?"

Oma nods, "yes, he did."

Erin is surprised. He bows at Oma, "You are welcome. Please be my guest." She blushes. Erin thinks he needs to get away from her, "Excuse me, I want to nap. Oma, please offer some water to them if they grow thirsty." He goes into the hut.

The young men are boisterous about their training activity. Someone goes to get drums, flutes and other musical instruments. They engage in fistfights and practices warlike dance steps.

Oma repeats some of the dance steps. They begin to play drums with hands and drumsticks. Oma excitedly dances around. She sees Ola and suspends one hand abreast her shoulder and the other above her head.

Ola is seductively dressed; her breasts are threatening to pop out of her tight tube dress. The way she impressively sways her hips turns the men's heart. The dramatists stop performing. They rush towards her and bend on a knee. Some of the men present an imaginary flower to Ola. Ola feigns acceptance of the gifts and sniffs the fragrances.

Erin comes behind Oma, "Is that part of the drama? It is quite alluring." He winks at Ola and the men.

Oma hastily turns around to face him, "Oh, you are awake. This is an unexpected twist to the drama. Obviously, the men are thankful for it."

Erin loosely crosses his arms on his chest, "obviously, they are lovesick. You should have given them such entertainment value before her arrival; you would have gotten flowers enough for a vase."

"Erin, keep quiet. I am a widow. Shameless," she moves few feet away from him.

Ola winks at Erin and sensuously walks towards them. She gently uses her hip to nudge Oma aside and stand by Erin. Erin moves away to create a distance between Ola and himself. He backs against a tree.

Ola smile sweetly, "hello, I am Ola."

"Hi Ola, I am Erin."

She hurls her short hair, "Yes, I know who you are. I have only not had the chance to run into you. Oma did not tell you I have always wanted to meet with you, eh. But hey, it seems today is a lucky day. I was passing by and bumped into you." She places her hand on the tree and thrust her breasts towards him that her nipples are slightly grazing his chest.

Oma is aghast at Ola's brazenness. "I will excuse the two of you," Oma flushes. She walks away to join the men that have continued their practice.

"Oma is very reasonable." She giggles. "Now that we are alone, I am wondering if we could get to know each other better." She fingers her waist beads and laughs huskily. "Erin, you're too handsome. I always daydream about your face. Now that I have heard your voice, I am sure I will be hearing voices in my sleep. The little sensible peace of mind I have will desert me today."

Oma pretends to be engrossed in the drama. She keeps stealing glances at Erin and Ola. Erin catches her gaze and she quickly looks away.

Erin gently pushes her aside and grins. They hear a clatter from the house.

"I think something fell down."

"There is no need to stress; it might be a silly rat running around."

Erin hands up frustratingly, "I need a confirmation."

Ola twists her mouth fast and shakes her head, "okay, come back soon," she scrapes his shoulders with her knuckles, "I am waiting." She slowly moves away from him.

Erin sighs and quickly walks into the hut. He picks up the fallen silverware from the floor and puts it on the table. He remains indoors.

Erin paces about in the room, he knows Ola is about to make tough advances at him. Erin hears footsteps. He runs and lies on the bed, pretending to be asleep.

"Erin," he hears Oma call him. She opens the door. He snores. "Oh, he is fast asleep."

"Wake him up; let us tell him we are leaving. I will wake him up." Ola steps a foot into the house and Oma mildly drags her out.

"Ola, please let him be. Can you tell me what the need of waking him up is? A sleepy head does not make a good escort. Let him have his rest. Come, hurry, we should be able to meet up the masquerades."

"Who cares about them?" Ola hisses and enters the house. Ola is walking towards Erin's bed when Oma grabs her arm and drags her out.

Erin opens an eye to see if they are gone. Oma catches him and the expression in his eye seems to say, *'don't you dare give me up to Ola.'* Oma chuckles and covers her mouth.

"What is it?" Ola asks.

Oma takes her hand, "It was nothing, let us go, Ola."

They leave. Erin hastily opens his eyes. He sighs with relief and gets up. Erin opens the window slightly to watch the women. Ola walks on carelessly. He chortles, "So she can walk that inelegantly." Erin smiles fondly. He thinks aloud, '*Oma you are such a sensible woman. Take that girl away from me, far away from me. May the gods add to your wisdom? Oh, yes they should. You just saved me from the seductress.'*

Ola falls on the ground and some of the men help her up. Maduve lingeringly wipes dust off her arms. Ola snobbishly takes his hands off her. She hisses and storms off. Erin chuckles and closes the window.

It begins to rain. Footprints of the visitors wash off from the farm. Indoors, Erin conjures fire on his arm and prepares a small hand-held pot of tea on the fire. The heat warms up the room. He sips the tea and stares at his wrist, "I wonder where Keme is? His absence is a great obstacle. What am I still doing here? I cannot wait to deal with that son of a serpent. I wish to get hold of him."

Erin groans loudly. Thunder reverberates in the sky. Erin relaxes. He smiles, it is calming to know his vehemence still boils hot and roam savagely.

Chapter Seventeen

Screeching bells cringe in the coven. A witch skins the dinosaur. She puts the peel in a medium size bowl and pours jar of murky water into the bowl. Another witch plucks out the baby dinosaur's eyeballs and put it in an hourglass. She put the hourglass beside the bowl. The skin dissolves into a sticky greenish substance and the eyeballs jump in the hourglass.

Keme and Cocovkpe come from the bedchamber. They watch Erin in the bowl of greenish water. She swims her fingers in the water. The image vanishes. She sucks her knuckles.

"Now you have your answers."

"So, this is what he is. He is not mortal. He is not of this world. No wonder he knew me to my bones." says Keme.

"You were lucky Oma stopped him. A single thunderbolt of his would have shattered you into pieces. He is Erin, the god of thunderbolt and vengeance, the successor of our Lord Eternal, Edion. Be thankful to Oma. Erin is as ruthless as his father." She shatters the bowl with clenched fists.

Keme whistles and curiously walks around her. He stops and picks a piece of the broken bowl. He studies it, "you are knowledgeable of Edion and the upper world."

"I was Edion's personal cleaner. I tended his chamber. I desired him. He loathed my love. It was the night of Erin's birth; Edion had too much wine and had his way with me. I allowed him because I loved him. I enjoyed the moment. He caressed me all over my body and told me how beautiful I was. It was my dream come true, to know Edion wanted me as much as I loved him. By morning, he realised himself; he was sober and blamed me of seduction. His anger left these ugly scars." She touches her face. Her eyes glint in anger as she recalls the scene.

Edion rouses from a trance. He scratches his eyes and is shocked to see Cocovkpe naked in his bed. He rests on his elbows, and asks her, 'How dare you sleep on my bed?'

'We loved each other all night,' Cocovkpe smiles nervously.

He slowly looks at his lower body, 'What have you done to me?' He angrily gets up from the bed, wears a golden mantle and screams; 'guards.' He grabs her hair and disgustingly stares at her, 'why did you dare?'

Cocovkpe quivers at the dangerous red flashes in his eyes. The angelic guards fly into the chamber. They bow and flap their wings. He instructs them to take her out of his sight.

She traces the scars on her face with a finger, "They dragged me out of his chamber. The whole kingdom witnessed my humiliation. He disfigured my beauty, took away my innocence and cast me to this barren land." She looks pained.

“You gave him your innocence. You have always been so cheap I guess,” Keme scoffs.

“How dare you?” She kicks Keme’s manhood. “I don’t think you are ready to get your reward,” she says and angrily walks away to sit on her throne.

He groans, “Ouch, I was only joking.” Keme hops to kneel in front of her. “I am sorry.” She looks away. “You hate him so much.”

She faces Keme and rubs the scars on her face with both hands, “I despise him wholly. However, my night with him was not useless. He had to kneel between my legs to seek pleasure. He bowed to me.” She laughs sinisterly, “That night was not in otiose. I sipped from his strength. I am glad I have some powers from him,” Keme looks very surprise. She nods, “Yes…because I shared body fluid with him. His fluid renewed me with powerful magic. My hate for him turned it into very dark sorcery.” The room becomes very dark. Evil sounds echoes around the coven. “I am gathering forces, angry women that have been stigmatised to torment Edion’s creatures.”

Keme grins wickedly and joins his palms, “Then, we have a common plot to execute, to destroy Edion and his entity.”

She gets off her throne, “Yes, and now his son is in our midst.” They laugh sinisterly. She takes the broken piece from Keme and magically couples the bowl. She uses her eyes to fill it with black water. “Come with me, I need to give you some of my innocence.”

Cocovkpe leads Keme like a sex slave. In her personal chamber, she pours bloody wine into two goblets. “Here is a toast to celebrate an impending doom.” They clink glasses and drink. Afterwards, they make love.

Kerhi comes out of his hut singing. He clears his throat nosily; adjust his wrapper and sits. He sniffs some powder, inhales deeply, whistles and slowly shakes his head to the intoxicating effect.

"Hmmm, this is good stuff. Good stuff, I am happy I changed traders. Ukovwe sells mild snuff to me and boast he mixes the best substance," he scoffs, "I will be buying from the new trader." He sits up and recalls the words he spoke to Erin.

He shakes his laps, "I was too harsh on him. Why have I been bothered? I know they like each other but Erin and Oma do not admit their love for one another. I think that settles the fact that they can manage their feelings even if they cannot form a union. I was selfish; I do not know much about him. He might have a wife and child somewhere." He hisses and crosses his legs, "Oh, curse my stupidity. He has a life before Igowe. I judged him too quickly and unfairly. They are cool with their slices of such fate. So why should I lose sleep over the issue? Kerhi, Kerhi, you meddle too much."

He sees his daughter come out of the kitchen. He beckons at her. Oma drops a basket of palm fruits on a stool. She wipes sweat off her chin with her arm and comes to her father.

She kneels before him, "Greetings father, how are you?"

"I am fine, my daughter. And how are you?"

"I am very fine, father."

"I am glad," he says. She stands and turns to leave, "eh, Oma."

"Yes father," she comes forward and folds her arms.

"How was yesterday's rehearsal? Will you be going over to watch the youths perform today?"

Oma smiles, "Father, it was great, the dance steps they are practising have never been seen before. The drama will intrigue the people. And yes father, I would like to watch them today."

"Okay good, I have something for Erin. When you're ready to leave, come to my room."

"Okay father," she leaves.

Oma is carrying a bundle. She hugs the package to her chest and smiles. She sees Keme's wife on the way and the smile slowly disappears.

Kimva smiles warmly and takes Oma's hands. "Hello Oma. How have you been?"

Oma ignores her greeting, "please leave my hands. As you can see, I am going somewhere."

Kimva let go of her hands. She walks pass her, "Oma, I am very worried. Please have you seen Keme, he has not been home for two weeks."

She stops, "Kimva, I should be the last person you should ask about Keme's whereabouts. Why should I know? I have no ties with that evil man. He and his kindred disgraced me out of my husband's house. I had to carry my daughter's corpse and bury it alone."

"Oma, I am sorry for all the vile accusations and the pains you had to go through."

"Kimva, I am still in pains. You do not expect I will easily get over the pain of losing my husband and children. There is also a slander to my character, and you think the pains will just refresh like the river?"

"I am so sorry, Oma. That was a bad scheming from who knows whom, why and how they did all those vile things to you. Keme was wrong for not standing by you, he was Omena's best friend, and most trusted family. Please, for my sake, do not take my husband's actions and inactions to heart."

"I have left Keme in the hands of a greater power; it is left for the gods to deal with him. If you must know, Keme is the mastermind of the evil that befell my household." Oma leaves her dazed.

Oma brings the bundle to Erin, therein are some new apparels. "Father has sent these clothes. He said you should make a choice. Erin, he said you have to pick one to wear for the festival."

"That is so generous of him, thank you, and him. They are all beautiful garments. It is hard to settle for one." He touches the lovely soft fabrics.

"Okay, I can leave them here and come back later, by then you must have decided."

"No, there is no need for stress. I will just take one. Alternatively, you should pick one for me. I will go with any you choose."

"Okay, hum, your eyes are beautifully colourful today, lovely brown," she looks at the fabrics for a while. Erin chuckles and changes his eyes to different shades. "You can't fool me," she says. Oma's choice is a matching colour to his dark brown eye pupils.

He takes it from her hand, "Thank you, you have made a wonderful selection," Erin clasps the fabric to his body and admires it. "I will try it on to see the fitting."

Oma is wide-eyed. Fearing he wants to try the clothes in her presence, she closes her eyes. Erin smiles and taps her shoulder. She opens her eyes and he gestures for her to turn around. She shyly goes out. Erin grins and ties the long wrapper around his waist.

"You can come in."

Oma comes into the hut, "you look majestic. The attire is your perfect colour."

"This is not my real complexion. I am a fair god. A bath in the pool of lavender tanned my skin."

"Everything about you is really not what it seems like."

"My heart is. Unfortunately, it is not visible. I love you very much."

"I should be leaving," she says quickly. Oma folds the clothes and tie it up to a bundle. "I will tell father you made a great choice," she laughs, "silly, he will know when he sees the returned attires."

Erin holds her hands, "Oma, don't you love me?"

"I am leaving." He leaves her hands and she hastily walks towards the door.

"Why then did you stop me from finishing off Keme?" She stops. "Keme, I have no idea of where he is. You torture me with your denial. The more you avoid me, the more I long for you. I look very foolish holding on for nothing. I must be a laughing stock in the upper world. It seems I have come to fool myself on earth. I have no regrets, I have no regrets." Oma leaves. Erin looks sad and pulls off the cloth.

Chapter Nineteen

It is the evening of the Igowe festival. The initiates fence the arena with fresh palm leafs. This is to prevent any unclean person to gain entrance and ward off evil charms. The young men have a final rehearsal behind the scene. They are anxious to be launching their performance. They wear costumes to masquerade as sharks and crocodiles.

The intimidating masks appear by the riverside. The villagers cheer them with applauses and whistles. They stand and sit in a semi-circular position, facing the shrine to have proper view of the Iben-the river god with the oldest man in the village presiding as Obo, a chief priest.

Erin arrive the venue and Oma sights him from the clog of women she is sitting amongst. Some maidens begin to nudge one another and whisper into Oma's ears for an introduction.

Ola is closest to Oma. "Oh, Oma, he is so handsome. Please can you talk to Erin for me? I really want him to be mine. I have tried so hard. I want to be his wife."

"Meet him yourself and tell him about your proposal. The last time I saw you, you were doing a great job at it."

Ola giggles, "I don't know what came over me. Was I seductive? I guess not, my charm did not hook him. I must have bored him to sleep."

"Better luck next time."

"Oma, please I have been begging you to intercede on my behalf or do you want him for yourself. I remember you slept at his house."

"No, I do not want him. Mind you Ola, there is no intimacy between Erin and I. We did nothing of that sort. What do you think of me? I am still mourning my husband and children." Oma realises she is talking loud and covers her mouth. She looks at the faces of the people around them. The women are engrossed on stage; they could not have heard her outburst. She speaks in low tone, "I do not want him for myself. Ola, how could you think that? I have told you, Erin and I do not have a relationship. He is my father's guest and it's normal for us to be together at some points." She grits her teeth and faces the stage.

"Then, introduce me to him. Tell him about my proposal. Let us walk up to him before he goes to sit at the men's area." Ola hastily stands and dusts her skirt.

Oma drags her down to sit and grits her teeth. "Stay here. I will meet him and call you to come over."

Ola nods. "Be fast about that, please." She pats her hair and adjusts her tube dress. She bubbles up and down her seat.

"Ola, behave yourself before people think you are going mad. The ceremony has not fully started so there is no excuse to why you are being so idiotically excited." She stands. "Here hold this, and keep it safe. The money for our market day shopping is in there," Oma gives Ola her purse to hold and goes to meet Erin.

Erin sees Oma coming towards him and he stride towards the men area. She hurries up to him, "Erin, please wait." He halts and she is speechless in front of him.

"Yes Oma. What is it? Why did you stop me?"

"I…I want to apologise."

"Okay. Never mind, but be rest assured Keme would not escape our next encounter. I will fulfil my duty and leave this earth."

"Erin," she wants to hold him but recalls they are in a public arena. She folds her arms and smiles warmly, "Erin, I am truly sorry. I shouldn't have stopped you from finishing him off."

Erin ignores her plea. '*If I accept her apologies, the wall I am building against my love for her will come undone.*' Erin thinks aloud as he walks away to take his seat next to Oma's father. Kerhi claps Erin on the shoulder. Erin nods at him and looks forward to the ceremony.

Oma sadly returns to her seat. "I saw your best shot. Sometimes, I wonder how we became friends. You cannot do this one thing for me. Oma, you have been married once. You might become a bride soon. What is your magic? Hello, are we wearing different perfumes? Nice call, '*I will call you to come over*' indeed," Ola hisses and rudely gives Oma her purse.

The masquerades come out of the sacred grove. The Obo leads the troupe of masquerades. They move seamlessly to the shrine and the Obo pours libation on objects representing all the gods, imploring them to guide the performances to a successful ceremonious conclusion.

Erin grins at the objects representing the god of thunderbolt and vengeance, "it holds no resemblance to me. Creative though." He studies the other objects and chuckles, "the goddess of harvest will turn red if she sees the statue of herself. There is no statue of Edion. Hmmm, they want the image of Edion to remain perfect in their hearts I guess. It would be sacrilegious to create a false god of their universe. Yes, there is no replica to Edion. The likeness of the supreme god is in their hearts." He nods and smiles.

"Erin, is everything okay?"

"Yes Kerhi, I am fine."

"I hope you are feeling the sensations of the festival. It will get more interesting."

"Indeed, this is more interesting than I thought." They smile.

As the procession returns from the shrine, some spectators quickly move out of the way. The masquerades are very aggressive. It is a rule that the masquerades are not to be touched. Their machetes posed to slash anyone who dares to come near them.

Each masquerade carries head masks, which represent the totem of their gods. Each clan or individual hails when they recognise the one, symbolised in their personal shrines. The totemic gods that inhabit the waters are Agbakara-crocodile and the Oloda-shark.

The mother oloda and children rise above the water. The tempo of the drums and songs increases as they emerge from the water. They are beautiful creatures wearing silk material with velveteen, tucked in from the waist down to the knee level.

The male oloda wears grey to signify old age, the female wears green, which signifies fertility and the children's dressing of yellow represents youthfulness. Their ankles beads make jingling sound as their white painted legs storm the ground. No one sees the sharks' legs touching the ground. The villagers can only hear sounds of walking.

The oloda walk in a rank of father, mother, and children to look for forages. They happily feed on smaller fishes in the river. Just when the olodas are set to embark on their journey home, they meet with their own fate. The agbakara, who is very famished comes out and is ready to feed on the oloda.

The agbakara crawls toward the olodas. The male oloda defends his family. They both are at loggerheads, a fierce fight for food and glory ensues. The oloda narrowly escapes from the mighty grip of agbakara and runs away with his family.

The Obo emerge and dance around, blowing white native chalk in the air, while he meditates and recites some incantations, "The forces that live in water are in agreement with other land forces. In the glory of this festival, may the gods bestow on man, potent charms to fight evil forces."

The villagers sing songs as the masquerades take turns, one after the other to dance and entertain them. The Obo returns and the lyrics rise into a fierce song accompanied with heavy reverberating drums. The Obo and one of the masquerades display the potency of traditional medicine. The Obo requests bottles from the villagers. Men and women drop all sizes and colours of bottles in a basket.

The Obo breaks the bottles, places the broken pieces on a mat and lay atop with his belly while the masquerades jump very hard on his back. They dance violently and the motion grinds the Obo's body harder on the broken bottles. The Obo gets up without any injury on his body. He prances about, proud of his valorous feat of exhibiting his great immortality. The people whistle and cheer him on.

As drums beat increase to a possessing tempo, the Obo and one of the masquerades display the potency of invisibility. They grab fearful children. The children scream for their parents to come to the rescue. Their mothers are frightened and run to their husbands and relations who assure them to keep calm.

The Obo and masquerades disappears with the children and reappear with them. The people happily shout at the magic. The mothers reunite with their children and keep them by their sides. The Obo and his apprentice exit while the masquerades follow.

Chapter Twenty

Today is Keme's initiation into the coven as the first wizard of Apele. His crown is a black crow and he sits on a lower throne designed with ostrich feathers, next to Cocovkpe. The witches dance around their thrones in celebration. Each kisses Keme on his feet. He is very proud of himself.

The witches bow and chorus, "Oh, wild wizard of Apele, we are loyal to your commands. Oh, wild wizard of Apele, we are loyal to your commands. Oh, wild wizard of Apele, we are loyal to your commands." They dance and fly around the thrones.

Cocovkpe is impressed, "Now Keme, you shall go to the water, the spirit of our water goddess is compassionate to our scheme. You will have a bath. In the next phase of your initiation, you shall have a bloodbath. Let us go."

A witch fling a black cloak over him, the junior witches lead the procession, Keme is in the middle, and the older witches follow. Cocovkpe eats many octopuses and disappears from the throne. The crow makes a hoarse clicking sound and look sideways.

The hallway darkens. As they walk, the black snakes crawl towards them. Keme grits his teeth and closes his eyes. Several snakes coil around his legs. He opens his eyes and sees the snakes riding up to his waist. He is about to scream, two witches hit brooms on his head and a crab plasters his mouth. Keme screams into his lungs. He shudders until the snakes clothe him.

The witches hold their brooms in front of them and cackle wru wru wru wru yeye yeye yeye wru wru wru yeye yeye yeye. The crow let out series of loud caws. Keme mysteriously finds himself at a river in Igowe. He looks around and does not find any of his escort. The last thing he remembers was riding on the back of a big python. Blood is all over his body and the crown is no more on his head. He holds his throat and croaks like a crow.

An octopus with Cocovkpe face appears in the river. She summons him with her limbs. He pulls the cloak and hangs it on a tree branch. He dives into the river and swims towards her. The water washes off the bloodstains. She uses her limbs to scrub the sticky stains. She flings him into the centre of the river.

While swimming, he sees a white bowl floating. A bloody bull's eye appears in the plate.

"Eat it," she commands him. He chews and swallows it. The further he goes, he finds himself deep in the river. He sees mysterious things that he could not tell what they are. She instructs him to eat any eye he sees in a saucer. The saucers glows in the water, its incandescence illuminate the water surface.

Keme has become bold and fearless in the water. He associates with demons that roam the water looking for avenues to inflict harm upon humankind. They advance; soon they will be loose upon Igowe to wreak havoc. Keme becomes an ancient serpent. His tongue sweeps some monstrous creatures into the forest. Keme transforms into a human with normal garment and fall like dark cloud into his hut.

Kimva is shocked to see him. She fearfully gets off the bed. "Where did you come from?"

"Lower your voice, I need some rest." He eyes her. "Why are you in my hut?"

"I didn't know where you were. I felt more comfortable sleeping in your hut."

"Okay, you can sleep here, but make no mistake of using your body to touch mine." Keme turns around and pretends to be asleep.

Kimva shrugs and leaves for her hut. Keme grins evilly.

Cocovkpe laughs sinisterly. Her limbs slap the water in merriment. The water boils. She stops laughing and begins to dance. A big monstrous octopus rises from the river. She bows to it. "Thank you, oh, compassionate goddess. Your alliance is priceless. Shoulder us when the war begins."

Chapter Twenty- One

An old woman faces death sentence for witchcraft. Erin horrifically watch as some people drag her with a rope tied around her neck. She falls on the ground and cries for mercy.

He rushes out of the farm and accost the chanting mob. “Why do you mistreat this poor woman? What is going on here, let go of her.”

The woman peers at her saviour with hope he rescues her. She grunts, “Please help, I am innocent. I am not a witch.” Some men kick her. She coughs and continues to cry, “do not kill me, I am not a witch.”

“Please let her go. She is in so much pain.”

“No, we will not, we must get rid of this evil in our land,” says the leader of the mob.

“What has she done to deserve this animalistic treatment?” Erin asks, but nobody is talking. “Let go of her, she is innocent.”

“Yes, she is an innocent witch. She has hidden behind her chopped claws for too long, her true personality is now obvious. We now know she is a witch. She has choked her loved ones with invisible long nails.” The leader of the mob says.

“Who are you?” Erin asks the leader of the mob.

“I am her son.”

Erin sighs, "just let her go. She is innocent."

A woman comes through the crowd, "Yes, she is innocent, she is not a witch. The community branded her a witch when the last of her eleven grandchildren died. Her children brought her before the throne, and the king pronounced banishment upon her and seizure of her lands, but the children said they wanted her dead so that she will not be alive somewhere and eat them up. They also called her younger sister a witch, she was stoned with rocks until her face was shattered and she died. Now, they want to do the same to my mother-in-law. She is innocent, why will anybody not listen and give her a chance to prove her innocence. Please spare my mother-in-law; she has never uttered dark sayings in anyone's presence or in solitude."

"Will you keep quiet? I think you're tired of being my wife." The leader of the mob says. He holds her hands, "it could be you're together in a coven. You joined her to eat my child. You killed our child." The woman shakes her head. He pushes her to the ground and some people pounce on her, "hey, let her be. Carry on with the execution. I will deal with her myself." He roughly drags her home while she kicks and cries.

"You heard what her daughter-in-law said. We should give the old woman a chance to prove her innocence," says Erin.

The new representative says, "Erin, we honour you; we believe you will respect our rubrics and let us carry out customs. Do not stand in our way, Erin, you are a visitor in Igowe, it would be best if you stay within your limits. Do not interfere in the decisions of the people and king." Erin nods and steps back in resignation.

The woman's eyes plead for Erin to do anything to save her. The villagers march on. They beat her with brooms and sticks until they reach the market square. Some young men gather to execute her. They pour lamp oil on her and set her ablaze.

She burns while shouting, "I am not a witch; I am innocent." The witnesses move backwards so that the rotating inferno does not catch them.

The old woman escapes. She runs towards the stream. The people chase after her. Thunder strikes and they run backward. She keeps running and clamping her body to put out the fire. The old woman heaves her lynching body and jumps into the water. The people reach the stream and did not have a glimpse of her. They think she has drowned.

"Let us leave; she has met a deserving fate."

"We should confirm if she is dead. She might be alive. We should finish her off."

"There is no need. Go to your various houses. The witch is down. If she resurfaces, we will do the needful." The people turn and leave in murmurs.

Underwater, Erin breathes into her mouth. He clothes them with fire. He had seen her running towards the stream. He had dived in and stayed under water. He was happy when the old woman fell in. He stops hearing voices and comes up to confirm if the coast is clear. He brings her out of the water and drags her into a safe nest in the bush.

He pumps her chest and sucks water out of her several times. She gushes out water and coughs. Erin rubs her palms and feet to inflict warmth. He carries her up and takes her to the farmhouse.

The room is light up with soft glow from a dying fire. Erin opens the windows, fresh air rush in and the old woman inhales a ragged breath. Her eyes flutter open. She turns and sees Erin. Her stare is full of thankfulness. Erin smiles warmly at her. She returns a weak smile.

She recalls how she almost died and tears slid down her cheeks. Erin comes to her side; he holds her hand and rubs her forehead. "The way your hand is rolling on my head eases my headache."

"Do not speak, just enjoy the feel." She nods and closes her eyes.

Few minutes later, she falls asleep. She becomes feverish. When he gives her some water to drink, she sips the water, shakes her head and says, "I am innocent, I am not a witch, my children believe me, and people of Igowe spare me. I am not a witch."

Erin stirs her; she is startled and sits upright. She moves to the wall, her hands shakily ward off Erin, "no, no, please do not kill me, do not kill me," she closes her hands over her face.

"Calm down, I am not your killer."

"You have come to take me to them, please do not take me to them, I am not a witch."

"I know you are not a witch, and I have not come to take you anywhere. You are in my house and I have been taking care of you." She remembers the hands that healed and soothed her, "I brought you out after you jumped into the water, and I was so impressed with your strength and determination."

The old woman flashes back to all that happened, “thank you, you saved my life.”

“Your life is in the hands of the gods, it was not your time, and your presence on earth is ordained by the angels of life.” The woman walks to Erin. She bends down to touch his feet. “No, please do not. You insult me by doing this.”

“You are my angel, my creator sent you to save me.”

“Do not bow before me. To live this long on earth, you have become more than a mortal. The people of Igowe were too blind to see this, you are just like the ancient of days, and only the pure at heart live this long in good health. Do not bow before me; send your gratitude and thanksgiving to Edion. I am just a handmaid of the gods.”

“May the gods bless you and fulfil all your needs, my child.”

“And may the gods always be with your spirit. Do have a seat. I made soup. I will feed you.” He feeds her and they talk about Igowe.

Oma comes to the farmhouse. She claps her hands and calls out to Erin. The old woman looks startled. He gestures for her to stay calm.

He goes out to meet Oma. “You are here.”

“Yes, I heard you wanted to save the witch. Erin, that was not right. You almost incurred the wrath of the villagers. What did you think you were doing?”

“Is that what brought you here? Oma, you came all the way to reprimand me?”

"No, I actually came to talk about Ola. She likes you; I hope you will give her a chance."

"She asked you to propose to me?" Oma looks away. "Oma, you know it is you I love. I cannot love any other. My time here is limited; I do not have time to court any frivolous maiden. I have love for you, but you feel nothing for me. Oma, do you not feel a thread of love for me?"

Oma holds Erin's hands, "I love you Erin. By the gods I have come to love you very much."

Ola hears this and stares at them with hate-filled eyes. She leaves noiselessly. "I suspected she will not speak to Erin on my behalf. I trusted her." Ola angrily storms off.

Oma let go of his hands, "But, Erin what is the use of this fleeting love. It will leave me broken hearted when you are gone. Gods and mortals are the water and palm oil; the oil will always sit atop the water. The oil just gives the water a little colouration."

"But Oma, when water and palm oil boils together, they mix and become a sweet soup. There is a possibility I may dwell on earth. It is possible I can remain in Igowe, other gods' base here."

"You are Erin, the son of our Lord Eternal. Will I not incur the wrath of Edion if I accept this union?"

"You face no danger; I am Erin, if there is any threat to our love. I shall face the consequences alone. Oma, give your love to me. Have no fear."

"I will think about it."

"Do not take too much time; your decision will decide my fate." They hold hands for a while and Oma leaves.

Erin is a little happy. The old woman smiles at him. She motions for him to come to her, "a god is in love with a mortal." Erin stops her before she bows to him.

"She heard us, we were too loud," Erin says under his breath.

"Are you Erin, the son of Edion?" Erin nods. "My god and saviour, thank you for saving me. Thank you, my Lord."

"Rest, you are still weak." Erin adds dried palm fruit shafts to the dying fire.

She is depressed over Erin's sad mood. "Oma, she is a beautiful and comely woman. Love shine in your eyes. I heard her strong emotion for you, it is in her voice."

"She confessed her love today." He blushes. "She needs time to accept hers and my love."

"Trust your heart, Erin, the voice I heard, is a woman that has already said yes to your proposal."

"I hope so, I love Oma very much, and I shall dwell in Igowe. I am confident that Edion will approve of our love, because this feeling is so right." Erin smiles lovingly.

The old woman nods happily and sits upright. Erin serves some brew and feeds her.

They hear some sounds. In an instant, the roof of the house is detached. The villagers surround them. Ola is shocked to see Erin feeding the old woman. "I saw Oma with him; I swear they were holding hands and confessed love to one another. They are lovers." The youths ignore her cry.

"So, this witch is alive. Erin, we warned you to stay out of our decision. You dared us, now you shall perish with her," Maduve charges at Erin with his cutlass.

In anger, Erin opens his palms; he slowly folds his fingers and the cutlass freeze in the air. Maduve could not move his hand. Others have little time to analyse the cause. They charge at Erin, with his hands he rolls mist and throws the mist at them. They move backward coughing and gasping for breath.

A man grabs the old woman from behind and he holds a knife to her throat. Erin stares at the cloud and his eyes turns blue. As the man is about to slit her throat, the cloud opens. With magic in his hands, Erin raises the old woman up and thrust her into the sky and the cloud closes straight away. Erin shouts in rage, his eyes turns bloodshot, his body sparks fire. Igowe vibrates, the people fall over one another. There is roaring thunderstorm and the rotation stops.

The people marvel at his powers. They all bow down before Erin. Maduve says, "Son of Edion, spare us for our foolishness. We dread your retaliation for what we have done. Do not spite us; hold your vengeance and thunderbolts from us."

Erin releases the cutlass and turns around, his back facing the people. He goes into trance. Ola runs and catches the cutlass before it falls to the ground. She lay on the ground and hold the cutlass above her chest. The people are openmouthed. She stabs herself before anyone could stop her.

Maduve screams and kneels beside her, "Ola, why did you do this, Ola please, fight to stay alive, I love you so much. You cannot leave me."

"So you loved me."

He nods, "yes, but I was too scared to approach you."

Ola laughs mockingly, "You are not my type of man. I would have rejected your proposal. Anyway, I cannot live. I betrayed my friend. Oma, she will be ashamed of me. Our god of thunderbolt and vengeance loves her so much. I have reached my limit today." She digs the dagger into her chest some more.

"Ola," Maduve pulls out the dagger and blood gush out from Ola's mouth.

"Thank you," Ola says to him, "Thank you for hastening my death. I am scared to be alive. I fear the wrath of Erin. He will not spare me." She points at Erin whose posture is against the people. "His vengeance will not spare me. His rage will consume me." She coughs blood and dies.

Erin is free from the trance. He turns around to see the people mourning over Ola's death.

"Erin, please Ola cannot die," says Maduve.

"I am Erin, the god of vengeance and thunderbolt. She is dead. The powers to bring one back to life is beyond me. I am sorry." Erin walks away.

It rains torrentially. Some men carry Ola away. They throw her body in the savannah. There is no shelter to shield Erin; he conjures fire around his body.

The rain stops. He walks through the farm and comes to stand by the river. He is unhappy the people know his identity. "Every time Erin exerts anger, the god of rainfall sends down its power to cool the earth. The sun shines heavily to dry Igowe, but who will quench this undying love I feel for Oma. I am now a prisoner of my own powers. The goddess of hope has deserted me. Oh, goddess of hope, where are you? Keme show thy self. I am powerless to find you." Erin kneels and hit his hand on the ground.

He returns to the farm. The villagers have built a greater house with surrounding tents. He nods gratefully.

"Please accept our sincere apology, do not take out your anger on us." They chorus. Erin does not say a word. They bow and leave.

He enters the beautiful house and finds Kerhi sitting on a golden chair. Kerhi stands and bows to Erin, "My Lord, Erin, welcome back."

"Kerhi, you are here."

"The news is everywhere. A great god is with us. You lived and shared meals with us; I never knew the god found my humble hut noble to dine in."

"My destination was your house. I have a task to avenge the injustices meted out to Oma."

"You came to earth because of Oma. My Lord, you can carry out your vengeance from any angle of the upper world. You did not have to step your holy feet on earth. I foolishly let you labour on my peasant farm. Pardon me my Lord, I am very sorry."

"I chose to be a peasant, and I will be until I leave."

"The people will not take it kindly. I will not allow you lift a hoe on my farm, and on any other farm," Kerhi bows and leaves. Erin is in deep thought.

The old woman tells Edion about everything that has transpired in Igowe. Edion is not happy. He summons the wise men and sorcerers. They silently discuss.

As an honoured guest of Erin, the old woman lives in the realm of Favour and Mercy. She becomes the chaperon of Damena. Her abode is close to the goddess of fertility. She hears every discussion between the goddess of fertility and Damena.

"Erin is not back yet; mother I grow weary, my wedding invitation is in the hands of every god in the kingdom. Any time I stroll out, they throw compliments of my upcoming nuptial at me. They praise my beauty and tell me how fortunate I am to getting married to Erin. Mother, I will be a laughing stock if things go awry."

"They shall compliment you on your marriage soon. Come on, you stress, it will tell on your beauty." Damena gets a head massage from the goddess of fertility.

"Thanks, mother. I feel a bit relieved. I will take a stroll around the kingdom."

"Okay, I will join your chaperon to knit a very beautiful dress. Do not stay out long."

The old woman shakes her head. She knows the marriage could not be because Erin's love for Oma will not bring him back to this kingdom. She knits Damena's wedding dress. The goddess of fertility instructs her to add more diamonds to the bust.

The goddess of fertility goes to check on the tree cubs in the den of birth. She feels the pulses with her bosom and nods satisfactorily. She returns to her abode and joins the old woman to weave seams around the wedding attire.

Damena walks pass purgatory. She hears someone call out her name. She slowly turns around and sees Agbavwo beckoning her to come close to the gate. She haughtily fans herself, "Agbavwo, have you lost your manners? I will be married to the heir very soon. Don't you ever summon me with your sinful hands again?"

"If you do not come closer and listen to what I have to say, then you can kiss your dreams of marrying Erin, goodbye."

The souls in purgatory gasp. Damena flushes with embarrassment. "You will pay for this insult. I will marry Erin. He is mine. He must fulfil the oath of the throne."

"A nuptial with Erin will not come that easy. You have to take him by force. There is a conspiracy between Erin and Edion. I heard he is on earth for a mission."

Damena quickly comes to the gate of purgatory, "Agbavwo, tell me what else you know."

"It is for your ears alone." Damena draws closer to him. He whispers to her, "It is written in Erin's destiny. That he will fall in love with a woman. That is not you, Damena. He will form a union with a woman on earth, she is Oma."

Damena's eyes narrows dangerously, "how sure are you?"

"I am an angel of destiny."

Damena scoffs, "an irresponsible angel of destiny. So how am I sure you are telling the truth."

"Because I have altered his destiny, I was very angry when Edion condemned me to purgatory. I bribed the pythons to free my arms for a while. Those creepy snakes wanted a favour from me. I have a penchant of swapping destinies you know," he chuckles and his eyes darkens, "they freed my hands and I visited Erin in his crib."

"So you are the cause, Erin will not get married to me?"

"I can reverse the destiny. That is if you are ready to cooperate with me."

"How do you intend to do that?"

"Come a lot closer, I will speak it softly into your ears."

Damena stands in contemplation. Agbavwo whistles and counts his fingers. She glances sideways and affixes her ear to his mouth. He mutters some words. Damena's eyes widen. She withdraws.

"Take this mirror. Henceforth, you can see everything Erin does. You will see the total truth of his destiny." Agbavwo nods and slowly retreats to the far end of purgatory in reluctant steps.

Agbavwo claps his hands loud enough to gain the attention of everybody, "All souls should gather around me." Some souls hurry towards him while others reluctantly walk.

"Yes Agbavwo, we are here. What does a condemned god have to say?"

"He will not have anything good to tell us. I am sure he is responsible for most of us being here today. He might have swapped our destinies to unfortunate fates which are why we are languishing here."

All the souls begin to murmur. The noise irritates Agbavwo. He claps his hands and stamps his foot at the same time. "Can you all be a little discreet? You are all responsible for your woes. It was the fate predestined, that I gave to you all. Maybe you should blame Edion. All the fates come from him. If he designs you perish, then you perish. Blame Edion and not me."

The souls murmur louder and chatter amongst themselves.

"Quiet all of you. Quiet. If you will like to get out of here, then I have a solution. Come closer." They murmur and walk forward. Agbavwo shouts, "Hey, I need an obtrusive crowd or else I will not tell you the solution." They stop talking. He beckons at them to come forward.

The people come forward. Agbavwo clears his throat and speaks softly. The people gasps. Few move backward. Many move closer to Agbavwo with evil grin. Agbavwo nods. They laugh sinisterly.

Chapter Twenty-Two

Oma comes to visit Erin. She brings food and a small jar of water. "The community now knows who you are. You are not just the handsome guest they welcomed into Igowe, they are happy a god is in their midst." She happily pours some water in a cup. She hands it to him.

"And you, Oma? Are you happy I am still here?" He gently pushes the cup aside and the water spills on the floor.

"Forgive me Oma."

"It is okay, I will clean it up later. Just have some water and then you can eat."

Erin nods and drinks some water, "Oma, I know you do not like my presence here. I have not seen Keme for a while; I am yet to exert my vengeance." He looks at her with pains in his eyes. "I will fulfil my oath very soon. I feel Keme is close. I do not know for sure."

"Erin, you don't have to wait on the cause of that. I will not keep you any longer. You may leave. I will deal with Keme. I free you from this task."

"Oma, never avenge a crime by yourself. You called on me, here I am. Leave the desire to avenge the injustices Keme has committed to

Erin. Vengeance is mine. I will repay Keme's evil deeds. I came down to earth against all odds. I am here because of ungodliness and unrighteousness of that one man, who by his unrighteousness beat humanity with cruelty. Let the day of wrath come in slow or fast pace, it will be a memorable day. Humankind will triumph over evil." There are heavy thunderclaps. Oma nods. She serves his meal. After he eats, she bows and takes her leave.

Oma reaches home. Kerhi is lying on the ground. Blood streams out of his nostrils. "Father, father, what happened to you," she drags him up and places his head on her thighs, "father, did you eat or drink anything?" Kerhi weakly points at his snuffbox, he sneezes violently.

Keme comes out of Kerhi's hut. He stands in front of them and gives an evil laughter.

"You, you are here?" Oma is shocked to see him.

Keme scoffs, "Yes, Keme is back."

"What have you done to my father you wild beast?"

"Nothing, I just gave him a spectacular portion of what he loves," Keme goes towards Kerhi's chair and picks up the snuffbox. "He changed his snuff trader, I was the new trader he has been buying the more potential powder from," he sticks out his tongue and laughs.

"Keme…" regrets fills Kerhi's eyes.

"Yes, say my name, Keme…Bleat my name like a goat. Meee...Meee…" Oma wants to get up and go at him, "no, no, no Oma, I advise you rock your father very well until he dies."

"Father, please stay with me." She gently puts his head on the ground and run to get hot water from the kitchen, "come on father, the water is warm. Drink it so that it can distil any poison in your body."

"Hum, poor Oma. You do not know what I have given to your poor, poor father. He cannot survive the venom of an ancient serpent, silly." Keme spits on Kerhi and some parts of his body begin to peel off.

Oma tries to clean the spittle on her father's body but the scales of her palm peels off, she jerks up Kerhi, "Father please," she uses two fingers to press his jaw open and pours some water in his mouth. The water slips out of his mouth and Kerhi breathes his last.

"Keme up, Oma down, now can you scream already for your boyfriend to come." Keme twists his neck. "Scream, Oma, scream." Oma cries out. "Yes, yes, cry louder. I want Erin to come to your rescue." Keme disappears. His evil laughter re-echoes as Oma cries over her father.

"E, Er…" Her voice is hoarse to call out to the god of vengeance. She sits and raises her knees up to her chin. She stares at her father and cries. The goats in the kitchen stop bleating. The cocks crows and run out of the compound. Everywhere is silent, grave silence envelopes the compound as tears cover Oma's face.

Erin leaves the house and meditatively walks until he enters the forest. On the far end is a river, small monkeys jump from tree to tree; the bigger monkeys climb down the tree and playfully graze their feet on the water.

He feels edgy, he tries to conjure fire, but his bolt does not protrude from his fingertips. He put down his hands and exhales. He plucks a thorn out of a flower and the sharp protective spine of the plant sting his finger. Erin annoyingly drops the stalk and scratches his hand on the nearest tree.

Blood drips from his finger. He spreads his palms, "Blood in my finger?" Erin is shocked, "I find this strange. Something must be amiss. I have a strange feeling in my belly." He rubs his chin and suddenly says, "Oma," his eyes widens, and he runs off.

He comes to Kerhi's compound. People have formed thin and large discussion groups. Some women console Oma. A man tells him how Keme killed Kerhi. "Erin, where is your fury?" he asks himself. His shoulders become limp. He goes to console Oma.

The inhabitants of Apele drink cups of blood. Under the cloak of darkness, Keme leads the pack of witches out of the coven and into Igowe. They inhabit the forest. Some of the witches inhabit the bodies of the baobab tree and the leaves whither.

Only one of the trees-uwara kept afresh, none of the witches could penetrate it because Erin's blood has dried on it. The small red-substance enables the tree remains alive.

They bury Kerhi the next day. For two days, it is either the women prepare meals in Oma's kitchen or they bring meals from their homes to feed her. They chat with her for a while and leave one after the other.

It is the fourth day after Kerhi's death. Erin comes to visit Oma. He is at lost for words. He is not one to give condolence to a bereaved.

"How are you, Oma?"

"Still coming to terms with my father's death and I am still missing Ola. Soon, you too will go from me. I will be so alone."

Erin hugs her passionately. He rubs her hair and kisses her roughly. "Do you think I will leave you? Oma, I have series of strange feelings these days. I don't think I am ever going to leave you."

"Erin, are you sure?" Tears fill her eyes. "Please, never leave me, Erin. Do not go away and leave me alone. I love you."

Erin smiles, "I won't leave you, Oma. I am always with you." They kiss. A little goat runs through their middle. Oma laughs. Erin cleans her tears with his hand. He kisses her forehead and carries her into her hut.

Night falls. Erin comes out of the hut. The consummation of Oma's flesh is evident in the way Erin smiles. He goes to the back of the house to fetch some water. He sees some black cats running out of the kitchen. He shrugs and goes into Oma's hut.

The black cats transform into witches. They have been spying on Oma and Erin. They fly back to the forest to give Keme the information. His evil laughter echoes in the forest and the witches cackle wru wru wru wru yeye yeye yeye wru wru wru yeye yeye yeye.

Oma and Erin cuddle. The lovemaking that began with joy will end in sorrow. What began in light will end in darkness. While the village sleeps, the witches hold meeting in the wake.

Erin's uncontrollable decision makes Edion a weak ruler. Many deities renegade against his rules; they do the opposite of his commands. Law and obedience is hard to reinforce. His angelic guards desert him. Many gods begin to leave the upper realm; the flesh of the world attracted immortality.

Damena steals the keys to purgatory from the god of death and resurrection. She unlocks the gate. Agbavwo and some loyal souls that have pledged allegiance to him comes out. Other souls run after them, they are excited to gain freedom from purgatory. Agbavwo and his companions roughly shove the remorseful souls into purgatory.

Damena, Agbavwo and the others besiege Edion's throne. Edion is brooding in front of the mirror at Erin and Oma's consummation. He instantly stands aloof and turns his head sideways. He compresses the golden ball and covers it with his fist.

As they close in on Edion, the old woman sneaks from behind his throne. The dove flies away. Edion opens his balled fist and light enters their eyes. Damena covers her face while Agbavwo tries to get to Edion. The shimmers deter him, Edion enters the old woman's womb and the lighting stops.

"Where is he?" Agbavwo shouts. "Search the kingdom for him and bring him to my knees." They search around for him and cannot find him.

"What are you doing here?" Damena asks the old woman.

"I wanted to ask you something about your wedding dress, the seam…"

"There shall be no wedding. Go to my mother, and tell her I have become the ruler of the kingdom." Damena sits on Edion's throne and the mirror disappears. Damena gasps. She relaxes, "it does not matter. Sound the heavenly gong. Let the people know they have a new ruler."

"Yes, Damena," Agbavwo bows and smiles evilly.

Chapter Twenty-Three

It is very dark. Keme and the witches storm the village. They use magic to set houses ablaze and the occupants run out in shouting cry. Everybody begin to run into the bush. Thousands of witches emerge and fire arrows. They aim their bow and shoot targets in the throats and hearts. They cackle victoriously and go for more kill. The people' races for survival become mad as they see their relatives and neighbours falling to death.

They run into the forest and become trap in it. The witches advance, invoking snakes and many wild creatures to surround the forest. The people look to one another for a way out. They are happy seeing some Igowe warriors come forward with weapons. Maduve is leading the men. They are shocked when their own begin to cut and stab them.

Cocovkpe appears in Oma's hut. Erin jostles awake. He sees the witch. "Cocovkpe," says Erin.

"Yes, my Lord. I am shocked that you know me. Did your father tell you bedtime stories about me? Erin, I see how pleasurably you carry out your vengeance." Erin clenches his fist. "I hope Oma gave her consent before you bedded her. She is sleeping like an innocent slut."

"How dare you?" Erin shouts and points his fingers towards

Cocovkpe.

She laughs. "Have you not noticed your fingertips are useless? The thunderbolts in your hands have lost their powers."

Erin takes a deep breath and opens his mouth. "Oh, poor Erin, do not stress your lungs. On the day you rescued that old woman, remember it rained. Before you clothed yourself with fire, some cells of your powers had already been washed off." Erin looks around the room. "You are all mine, Erin. My war witches are in the forest dealing with the people of Igowe. Can you guess who is leading them? Keme, the one you seek."

"Ah." Oma screams and attacks Cocovkpe with her claws.

"Oma, I thought you were sleeping," says Erin.

"I have been awake listening to this witch."

"Get away from her, Oma; she is too powerful for you."

"Go, Erin, save the people."

"Oma," he comes towards her.

"Go Erin, save the people from Keme's evil." Erin nods and runs out of the hut without looking back.

Cocovkpe pushes Oma to the end of the room, "you think you possess some powers. You bedded the puppet heir. I sucked prowess from the throne itself." She charges at Oma. Oma looks around and sees a bowl. She smiles and quickly grabs the bowl. As Cocovkpe comes closer, she flings the content of ground pepper into her face.

Cocovkpe thrashes around the room, "how dare you, you little whim," she transforms into a hawk, flaps her wings and disappears.

Oma takes time to catch her breath, she throws the empty bowl away and slid to the floor, "Erin," she stands and run outside. There is no animal in sight. She rushes into her father's hut and grabs some daggers into a bag.

Erin goes to the farmhouse. He gets the golden pot and opens it. There is lightening in the pot. He opens his mouth and golden sparkles slouch down his throat.

Oma did not have to sneak into her former marital home. The whole village is deserted. She takes some of Omena's prized swords from his wall of fame and flees to the forest. Erin meets her at the entrance. They nod and vigilantly walk into the forest. The goddess of hope appears and follows behind. She flies ahead of them to give light to the forest.

Erin sees her and gratitude surge through his face, "I thought you deserted me."

"I had to attend other kingdoms. It is not easy to give hope to both gods and humans. Go on Erin, I cannot hold this light for long. Cast out darkness and bring back natural light to Igowe."

Erin nods to Oma and they begin to run. Oma throws two swords at Erin. He feels the weight of the swords and smirks, "Thank you my brave lady."

"You are welcome my Lord." Erin looks ahead. Oma keeps staring at him. The goddess of hope snaps her fingers at her and Oma blushes.

There is lighting, thundering, and whispering voices. Fire engrafts the forest. Flowers begin to grow thorns; the trees grab some villagers and dig its sharp stems into their flesh. It is a sight of horror, the victims scream in anguish. The thorns grow longer and wrap some people' necks until they gasp and give up.

Oma and Erin run in misdirected paths that take them into different parts of the forest. Erin sprays fire and releases thunderbolts on the witches. He uses the sword to fight Maduve's men.

Oma sees Maduve stabbing a child. She shouts in anger and topples his blade with her sword. He falls, "get up and fight," Oma raises her sword with one hand. He rolls on the ground and grabs his sword. He gets up and charges at Oma. They fiercely combat.

"You turned against your own people."

He cuts her on the jaw, "Yes I did. You turned into Erin's woman and I lost Ola because of that. How can I call the god of vengeance on a woman he loves?" He cuts her arm.

"You have no defence in turning against your own people." She rubs her face with her palm. He takes advantage of Oma looking at her palm and race towards her. She bends and he jumps over her. Oma quickly gets up before he lands. She takes him by surprise and cuts off his head. She pants heavily and spits on him.

Tension cracks begin to appear on the earth's surface. A volcano erupts which actively split the villagers on two sides. Cocovkpe cuts her vein with her teeth and her blood drips to form a red river in the forest.

Erin sees the divide and stops running. He tries to catch a child from slipping into the centre but he is late. Many people fall into the burning rift. Those that fall into the red river choke and drown. Erin conjures a candle and lights it. Purple candles appear in everybody's hands to repel the raging storm of the red sea.

Tornado rises and squeezes through the widening cracks, sometimes to erupt and form dark fog. Erin steps close to the rift zone to stop another rising tornado from erupting, but it still puts pressure on the crust and causes more fractures on the earth.

The tragic incident rustles the people. Many have died while others say their last prayers. They pray the gods spare them from total destructions, or that they have tender deathblows from the horridness that surrounds them.

Erin controls rocks and giant trees to fall into the rift. When the rocks and timbers fill up the crack, the people gasp and smile.

Oma comes to his side. "Erin, the destruction is chaotic, what do we do? How do we get out of here?"

"Follow me," he says. They carefully walk on the sealed earth and go towards the stream.

A voice speaks from the water, "the water deities will not have humans march on their faces. We are in a reflective season and would not entertain any disturbance. Those on land walk on land. In this moment, have contentment with the deities of the earth."

Erin turns around and signals to the people to halt. "You all wait here let me see if there is a way we can get out of here." He walks closer to the stream.

Oma holds his hand, "But we will perish if we cross this water; the water deities have instructed us not to disturb their peace."

"That voice is not from the realm of the waters. Oma, do not believe every spirit you hear and see. These are perilous times. We have to be careful. You do not have to go with me. I will save the peers of the kingdom. Many have died. If we do not take drastic measures, humanity will perish in Igowe. Oma, nothing will be left of you and your kind in this territory. Wait here, I will take the first step."

She takes his other hand, "You know that is impossible. For our love, I will walk any depth and length with you. What makes you think I will let you go alone? At this time, I wonder why I fell in love with a fool as you."

"Yes, my sensible warrior queen. Know that no harm can come to me. I am Erin." She smiles courageously and he squeezes her hands reassuringly. "No matter what, trust me to keep you alive, I cannot assure your safety, but I will lay down my life to keep you alive."

She slowly let go of him. "I know Erin, I know, but Erin, water weakens you."

"Don't be afraid. I have cloaked myself within. I am fire. I can never run out of my own spirit." Erin uses a foot to test the depth of the water.

"Please, be careful."

Erin nods; he enters the water and releases thunderbolts that kill all the wild evil creatures in the water. "Let us go."

The people enter the water and swim over to the mountain.

Oma stays behind. "I am scared of the water."

"Tell me you're joking, your father was a great fisherman."

"But he never took me to go fishing. I tried time and time again for him to take me so that I could get over the fear but he always told me it was dangerous."

"But you fetch water from the stream."

"I just have to stay by the river and fetch water in my pot. I am really scared." She shivers.

"Oma, few minutes ago, you promised to walk length and depth with me."

"Stop joking, Erin." She wraps her arms across her bosom.

"Okay, we will take another route, come with me," he takes her hand. They stop at a cliff.

Oma shakes her head slowly and steps backward in fright. "If this is the only way out, then let me die here."

Erin opens his palm, "trust me, Oma."

"Erin, I trust you with my life. But this is too much."

"Take my hand if you truly love me."

She walks forward, "Please, do not test my love with this depth."

"Take my hand, Oma, please." Erin looks deep into her eyes. She takes his hand and become lost in his gaze.

"With you, I am not really afraid."

"I will hold on to your words," he lifts her and she voluntarily wrap her arms around his neck. Erin jumps off the cliff without warning.

Oma screams and hides her face on Erin's chest. He lands and kisses her forehead. Some people are still crossing the water. Those on ground cheer Oma and Erin. Oma nudges his chest with her arm and he puts her down.

An octopus emerges from the stream and flings Oma against a baobab tree. "You cannot easily defeat me," says Cocovkpe. She laughs sinisterly and flaps her eight limbs. She dives under water.

Erin sees Oma falling from the baobab tree. He drops his swords and race in mad sprints, shouting Oma. The tree vibrates; dropping leaves that transforms into thorns as they touch the ground so that when she landed, the greenish spikes protrude every part of her body. Oma's eyes widens in helplessness.

Erin reaches her side and beholds her eyes turned bloodshot. In their depths, he sees Oma slipping away from him. Oma breathes thinly. The forest becomes green. The thorns change into leaves and retreat from Oma's body.

"Erin, I lo, ve, I love yo, you."

Erin lifts Oma from the ground. He walks towards the temple of Igowe, and lays her on a hammock held by the teeth of four wild beasts.

Erin prepares to perform the owenurhomu-to exchange his life with Oma. He wants to direct her death to himself.

The temple beholds a burning furnace; Erin takes an oil lamp and empties its content into the furnace. He conjures a pure candlestick and lights it from the furnace.

He walks back to the hammock and undresses Oma while he silently moans. He lifts the candlestick that has burned to half. He turns the candle upside down and each melting wax falls on the wounds. He cuts his vein and golden fire flow out of his wrist onto her slight opened mouth. As it drops, the wound neatly heals and the scars vanish.

"Oma, like burning coal of fire, this fire bright and sacred is an exchange of my majestic seat. I give up my strength to find an eternal space here. This bright fire is what is left of my immortality. You will awaken from the cold of death, and I shall be reborn with the fire of life, I will be a living fire and I will incarnate to replace the fire of Igowe that burns through the hearts of many that abound in this kingdom. This sacrifice is a symbol of my love to you. For my love for you, I become the dragon of Igowe."

Oma slowly comes alive, and Erin gradually evolves into a dragon. As her eyelids flutter open, the dragon dive into the burning furnace and all of sudden the temple is light up in golden shimmer.

Oma calls out to Erin and the furnace breathe a ferocious fire and roar in anger. She stands and goes towards the furnace. The roof of the shrine split and a great star fall from the cloud. It transforms into Erin's staff of thunderbolt, burning as a lamp, it rises from the ground and dives into the furnace. The fire roars consistently.

"Erin, you left me. You left me." She falls to the ground and sobs into her palms.

The villagers see lightening and hear heavy roar. They move backwards and stand afar from the shrine. They expect the heightening fire to engulf the shrine but they are shocked when Oma comes out naked. Some women scramble towards her. They use their shawls to clothe and take her away.

The sun ceases to shine and the moon is scarce. Starless nights after nights, the people mourn the tragedy that befell the land. There are storms. Hazards and blisters cover their bodies. Shrine of Igowe boost with raging flames, those who surround it, keep warm by its spiritual heats.

The goddess of hope appears and twirls her wand. The earth and water get into a fierce battle, as they whirled together, faster and feistier; dust and splash of water kindle and rips into the air, a spark of life rests on the doomed kingdom with rare hope. After the battle, there is an enormous darkness, the monstrous shape rise above the earth, roaring into the cloud and the land boosts with sun.

The vegetation begins to grow lush and the forest grows dense and steep. The people are thankful to the gods for savaging their land and restoring lost hopes. The sunshine and rain upon their fields are immeasurable.

Once again, they worship 'Edion', they create sacred groves and sanctuaries they will offer praises and perform daily rituals to appease the souls that are gone to keep great watch over them, and never allow such ills to befall them again.

Oma is miserable living all alone. She goes to the shrine of Igowe. She rests her back on the wall and cries while the fire begins to roar recurrently. She cleans her eyes and pants heavily.

She runs towards the river, behind the shrine and contemplates on jumping into the water, "let me end it all," she hiccups. "I am so unlucky to find lasting love. None of my love survived. I will drown and kill this pain forever," she sniffs and uses a hand to wipe the tears on her chin. "Nobody will miss me, nobody." She spreads her arms and places a leg forward.

Fire razes out of the furnace and plunges into the river. The water dries up the moment she falls into it. Some men jump into the deep and one of them carry her out. She has fainted and injured her arms.

They take Oma to her house and some women come to nurse her with massages, entertaining camaraderie and good meals. But Oma still has sad looks in her eyes and dark smiles on her lips. She faints. The women finds out she is with child.

Many moons have passed. Oma could not muddle through the stages of her pregnancy alone. She can hardly sweep the compound, prepare her meals, and work on the farm.

Some women send their children to fill her pots with water. The people are not malicious towards her as a widow with child because she is carrying the seed of a god. Oma sends words to Gwons. Her aunt and Madu come to take her away to live with them.

On the road, her water breaks. Oma begins to have contractions. Madu goes in search of a shelter. He finds an old farmhouse and they bring Oma to it. She cries due to the series of spasm that heebie-jeebies her body. Umota delivers Oma of a baby boy.

Oma laughs and cries happily when the baby will not stop wailing. She wipes her tears and pulls down her wrapper to let her baby have suckles. Her aunt cleans her up with some wet soft wrappers while Madu goes to tend the donkey.

Chapter Twenty-Four

It is now seven years since Oma and her son moved to Gwons. Madu has grown from a young lad into a handsome man with moustache.

Gwons is a blessed village with species of cash crops such as palms, cherry, orange, mango and mahogany. Others include rubber, kola nut and cocoa. Major food crops cultivated in the land are cassava, plantain, cocoyam, maize, yam, pepper, melon, vegetable among other farm products. The people produce Amivi (local body cream) and Oza (soap) which they sell and use at home.

Some individuals have large rubber plantations, which they either tap or hire out. Tappers sell the rubber produce to merchants in forms of rubber lumps and sheets. The merchants in turn sell to the factories where the products are refined.

Few people engaged in cocoa production, while others are involved in crafts. Those who engage in cocoa farming harvest and dry the seeds for sale.

Artisans weave ugẹn, akẹdẹ, ikidẹn, aharọ (fishing tackles), okalokpọ (basket), atẹtẹ (local tray), ophorho (garri filter), ere, odjiko, abiba (variant mats) and aga (chair) for sale and it has great rivers for fishing.

Madu comes early to the river to catch fishes before the women and children come to upset the water creatures with flurry of activities. His net was fortunate to catch big fishes despite the rough mending it had undergone the previous night.

Madu feels uneasy. He is in haste to round up his fishing. He goes to his farm to pick up some cocoyam he has harvested earlier. He straps the basket full of cocoyam to the rear of his bicycle, and securely ties it. He usually finishes his day tasks before sunrise. He mounts the two cycles in brooding silence. He wonders how is father fared, his health has deteriorated since the last full moon.

Madu rides out of the farm. His cousin runs towards him. The seven-year-old boy is barefooted and his face flushed from the exercise.

He holds the basket and tries to catch his breath, "brother Madu, brother Madu. Come quickly, grandpa, your father battles with his soul. The angel of death is choking him. Hurry brother, hurry," he hit the basket.

"Oh, my god…" Madu quickly comes down from the bicycle.

"Be fast, brother Madu, grandpa…" The little boy urges him to come down from the bicycle as if his quicken steps could save the old man.

"Come on, take this." Madu offloads the basket on the ground and gestures to the boy to bring it to the house.

"Can you carry it?" He lifts the basket and put it on his head. Madu nods and runs off.

With the weight on the bicycle reduced, Madu is able to ride lightly with a heavy burden lapped in his heart. He reels the wheels as fast as his heart could carry him to his father's bedside.

Squirrels scamper from the road track as Madu speeds through the neatly cleared bush path being careful not to trample on any of the squirrels having a field day in the cool atmosphere. After riding for about thirty minutes, he reaches the spot where three junctions meet and hears three booms in the air.

Madu with his bicycle crashes to the ground as the meaningful sound confirms his worse fear. Madu cries out in the serene environment. A goat stares at him. The goat bleats it annoyance at the disturbing sound Madu is making, and returns to munching his meal of fresh cassava leaves.

Madu stands and cleans dust off his cloth. The goat moves to another portion of stem to eat some more leaves and irritatingly moves away from the bereaved man.

Madu rides and parks his bicycle at an old Igbedin shrine to continue his journey on foot. His shoulders slumps, "there is no need to hurry. I will only behold a corpse when I get home. My father is gone from this fleeting world." He strolls home in a dark mood.

Oma and his mother are crying. He walks straight to his father's hut. He kneels beside the corpse and cries silently.

"Madu, be strong. The women must not see you crying. You have to be strong. Do not mourn like the women. Dry your tears and go out to console your mother," the native doctor packs his medicine bag, "I tried all my skills of healing, but I could not save your father." He pats Madu on the back. Looking up to the roof, he sighs deeply and leaves.

The boy reaches the house. He sees his mother and knows the worse has happened. He goes to sit beside his mother and takes her hands.

Oma looks at him, "we lost him, Erivwa. Grandpapa is gone."

Erivwa wipes his mother's tears and sits on her laps. She hugs him and sobs on his shoulder.

Madu dozes off on the corpse. He has a nightmare and wakes before a beast caught him. He pants unspeakably. He stands and leaves the room to join the others.

Chapter Twenty-Five

Madu slowly wakes, bed bath in sweat. It has been six months since his father passed away. The nightmare he has had on the day of his father's death persists. The shadow of the monster comes afresh in his sleep, night after night. Today, he has seen his father in his dream as well. His father has tried to feed him meat. He guesses his refusal to allow the beef pass through his lips, is what has woken him.

Madu picks up his old slate and cleans off dust on it to reveal the faith he has embraced against his father's wishes. Some ineligible texts are on the slate. In the heat of their conflict, they had quarrelled for days and then his father had contracted an unknown illness. The mystery of the strange ailment still baffles him. He calls out Erivwa to bring him a cup of water.

"Hope the water is as fresh as spring," he asks taking the cup from him.

"Yes, brother Madu. It could not be fresher than the dazzling spring water. Still it is as cool and dazzling as its source, our fountain of life- the great river of Gwons."

Madu laughs and drinks some water, "Ah, I feel I've drunk directly from the cool refreshing source indeed." He gulps the rest of the water and ruffles Erivwa's hair.

Madu steps out of his hut into the brightened sky and stretches his hands. He gives a little shake to his waist and flexes his shoulders off fatigue.

"Guess what, brother Madu," Erivwa says from behind.

"What is it, boy?"

"Just guess," Erivwa grins.

"Erivwa, you are getting too smart. Do you want me dehydrated from asking questions and guessing? You should not have given me a drop of water, then. You know too well, I am not good at guessing. So, come out with it. Come on, tell me." Madu tickles Erivwa's armpit to wriggle the words out of his mouth.

Erivwa laughs hysterically, "Okay, okay, I could swear I saw the river goddess sitting by the riverbank the previous evening." He touches the emerald locket on his neck.

"Was our Ehiri not by her side, playing the flutes for other bevy of beauties of the sea?"

He snaps his fingers, "the gods forbid our Ehiri will stoop that low."

"Same way I didn't expect you to stoop this low that the mermaid will visibly appear to anybody. Now, shush your mouth and get along with your chores. Bring me my fishing net by the kitchen. I hope it's dry?"

"At once, brother," Erivwa runs off playfully and returns with the fishing tools. "Will I eat the meat you caught yesterday?"

"No, you will not."

"But brother Madu, you promised I'll get a treat from your trap, today."

"I also caught fishes with my traps. Trap is trap."

"Brother Madu please, I'm begging for just a piece, let me have a taste of bush meat. Mother doesn't feed me with it; I only get the taste in the soup."

"You know what they say about these edibles. Eating eggs will make you steal."

"And the consumption of snail will make the child salivate excessively."

"Good boy, you know the rules so well. In that case, do not waste your energy in begging for what you will not have for now. It is a taboo for children to eat meat. Your mother did not eat it while she was pregnant with you, not even eggs. I have seen you salivating at the hen lately. Erivwa, don't you dare pick up an egg once the hen lays her eggs."

"I want to eat egg and be brave and strong like you. I want to be hard working."

"You will be, my boy; it is just a matter of time. Eating big meat and eggs will make you steal, the gods will surely punish you for stealing, and that will not help you be great in life. Mighty drops make an ocean."

"But with a big fetcher, I can hasten up and fill up the ocean."

"With what strength will you use to carry the fetching pail?" His shoulders drop and Madu ruffles his hair. "Slow down, my boy."

"Okay," Erivwa beats his chest and smiles.

"Go and do your chores. I need to sleep some more. I was restless last night."

"Okay, brother Madu," Erivwa runs off and takes a broom.

Madu goes into deep thoughts. Oma shakes his shoulder, "I've been talking to you, but it seems you haven't been listening. Your mind has journeyed far to another world."

"Sorry Oma, when did you come? I did not hear the sound of your footsteps. Please, take a seat."

"Madu, what is your problem?"

"I don't have any problem."

"I see." She takes a seat.

"Okay, I will tell you. These days, I am gravely disturbed. I wonder how I will contact my dead father. I need to know why he keeps appearing to me. He always tells me to seek him out."

"There is a medium I know."

"What medium?" Madu twists his moustache.

"It is known to only those who want to find solutions to their problems."

"Yes I have a great problem." He says urgently. "I need to know where I can find answers."

"Oh, now you agree you have a tough problem. I shall point the direction where you can find the palm reader. He is a great soothsayer. But be ready to travel a great distance."

"But who can contact dead people?"

"He is a great seer. He can connect to all spirits, except Edion. Born blind and crippled, he sees and walks more than any man or woman that ever lived in this kingdom."

He rubs his chest. "My spirit forbids I embark on this journey."

"But you seek answers."

"Oma, how do you know this great seer?"

"Don't be silly. This is my maternal home." Oma playfully slaps his cheek and leaves.

Madu does not know there is such things as communication with the dead, but because of the disturbance from his father's ghost, and the word 'set the light free' that keeps echoing in his ears at night. He decides to seek the sorcerer. He may lose his sanity soon, if he does not find a solution. He needs answers. "Perhaps, the sorcerer will be able to tell the fortune of my future. Although I know, I will prosper in my fishing and hunting games way beyond what I am expecting. I have to seek the sorcerer." He sighs and closes his eyes.

Chapter Twenty-Six

The sorcerer's hut is atop a gigantic hill, clustered by wild forestry. When the village had had a bloody clash with its neighbour, the mountain proved a safe harbour. Only the resilient, dared to make it to its opened galling entry point. It was a cold war, from land to water, through air and invisible trails. So many lives taken and casualties left to mourn losses. At the foot of the hill lies the well of death. The villagers had dug the earth a hundred feet deep to trap their opponents and the skeletons of the enemies will dwell in the well forever.

Severely disturbed, Madu reaches the mud stairs that leads to the great seer. The constant dreams leave him no other choice but to seek answers as to why his father's spirit would not rest in peace.

The sorcerer is seated, legs crisscrossed with calabashes turned upside down at both ends of his feet. His long grey hair falls loosely around his shoulders and covers his face, giving him a wizardry posture. He slowly nods to acknowledge Madu's entrance.

Madu bows, wondering how the blind old man senses everything around him. He hangs his hunting gun by a nail to the wall and walks noiselessly into the room to make himself comfortable in like manner of the sorcerer, only that he places his hands in an opened calabash that suddenly fills up with warm water. Madu exhales loudly as the effects calmed his troubled soul.

"I see the turmoil in your heart. Darkness wages war in your eyes, so much that your sights only behold bleak darkness with no shaft of light. It is good you've found your way to your deity's cave."

"Wise one, I'm glad that you can see through my happiness, the sorrows that lies within; you see my pains of many nights and days. I ask therefore, what can still the storm of this steel that makes mockery of my daily life and inner peace. Sometimes, I don't know if I should just plunge into the river and just drown it all."

"Even if you seek death so dearly, it will shy away from your miserable helplessness. Shame should string your tongue for such utterance; those are words of wretched cowards."

"Wise one, forgive my unruly tongue, so uncouth in the realm of wisdom."

They stare at one another, eyeballs to eyeballs. Madu is the first to look away as the intensity from the sorcerer's lifeless eyes burns into his.

"Tell me, wise one. What do you see in my soul?"

"I could not see pass your flesh. You will have to come another day for the revelation."

"But wise one…"

"You are still a coward, who is not ready to see the truth. Your eyes cannot see through the revelation from the gods. Your ancestors retreated when you looked away."

"Wise one, the intensity in your eyes burned me; they caused me to look away."

"Those were not my eyes. It was the fortress of your ancestors. You are not ready to find out what plagues your homestead. Your heart is fickle and your sights are cowardly. When you can stare undauntedly into the eyes of your ancestry, only then would you be privy, and worthy to learn of the sacredness that surrounds the mystery of your father's ghost."

"But wise one, how will I ever dare to stare point blank at my ancestors? Are they with clothes or in flesh? Are they not in naked form, which is one reason, a child, cannot grace their glory? Am I doomed not to find solutions to these troubles? The depths of my ancestor's thundering eye sockets will surely electrocute my entire being; it will certainly be my ruination. It will mark my end."

"Then so be it…"

"Wise one…"

"You sound too much of a coward. I wonder how a lion gave birth to a squirrel that scurries about bush paths and tree branches. Oh, he that sends hearts to the sun, how did you sire a wavy shadow."

"Wise one, I shall overcome, beseech the gods and my ancestors that I overcome all these cowardly forwardness."

"Go to your shrine; rehearse on the stool faced to your ancestors.

Then, you can call back to the deities in order to conquer your fears and ride to the path of discovery."

"Yes, wise one."

"Madu, you shall conquer fear, for the good and grace of your beloved." Madu bows and leaves.

Nipa comes to enjoy splendour of the noon heat. Madu is wandering in the farm when he hears a faint song. He walks towards the stream, parts some flowers, and sees her bathing and dancing in the water. Her mellifluous voice mesmerises him.

Upon sighting Madu, Nipa places her chin on her palm, exhales towards him and looks up to the sky. Instant dumbness does not afflict him and this surprises her. No one gazes at her nakedness and remains whole. She strangely looks at Madu, expecting madness will strike him so that he will never make a sane statement that people will believe.

"Who are you? My annoyance has made you neither dumb nor mad. I should paralyse you from head to toe. You would be rendered useless for life."

"My little cousin has seen you. He was unaffected. I am his elder, why should I not be stronger?"

"I shall peel off your skin," she angrily slaps the water with her foot, the liquid spirals and it slouches over Madu. However, he remains unaffected. Nipa sighs and combs her hair with her fingers. Her beauty infatuates him. He fixes his gaze on her milky flawless skin.

Nipa removes large branches of leaves with her cool blue eyes and covers her naked form. She stands and majestically walks towards Madu. She besots him with a sly smile that makes him feel as if he has fireflies in his heart. He clutches his heart and inhales slowly.

She drags him to the stream and makes him lie on the lush flowerbed. She is on heat to mate with the human that dares to look upon her nakedness and remained sane.

"You are precious," Madu cups her face as she lies on him.

"And you're bold upon the streams I have my bathing ritual. How dare you?" She brushes his lips with kisses to stop him from replying.

"I've been told you reign over our lakes, and sit upon the riverbank at leisure, but I thought you were an imagination. It is wondrous you preside over the stream in fresh and luscious physical form." He holds her waist.

"And you seem like the river god, embodied with the river's spirit, all the ancient spirits that inhabit the still waters of marshes, ponds and lakes are present in your body." She massages his body very hard. "Yes, I feel the strength of immortality in your spirit. I've longed for the one who compliments me, little did I know, he would grace my presence today." They kiss. "I have hoped on many nights and days, to find one in all the earth's water system, in this sea deep in cavernous spaces, my wonder overlaps in this little gracious pond. I am glad I had my bath in this beautiful spring in the mash of subterranean flows from Gwons. I found you. You're so daring."

She blinds him and they make love. Madu does not see the contented expressions on her face but he feels the sensuous twist of her body on him.

"My name is Nipa, a princess of the sea. You may not regard me in the highest order because I am a shameless seeker of pleasures, but not any man thrills me, my fondness of love is comfortable with your spirit. Will you love me? I know I'm not chaste but…"

Madu stops her words with a finger on her lips, "I do not doubt your dignity. Your pleasures are refined for the finest, you found me worthy, just as you are a gem to me. Never think otherwise, Nipa, you are my goddess and I cherish you with pride."

They smile at one another and detached. Nipa slowly stands, twirls and dives into the river. Madu walks home whistling with contented look in his eyes.

Nipa and Madu secretly see one another in the stream. She is impatient to make love to him whenever they meet. On one of their meeting days, Madu is not forthcoming and she misses him.

She decides to go into the village and look for him. By the bush path, she sees Madu with another maiden and goes into a rage of jealousy. The maiden is shocked to see such a fair goddess before her. Nipa assumes she is Madu's lover and leaves.

In her jealous antics, Nipa makes the river turn red. She tells herself she will not accept any of their sacrificial offerings. She slowly puts a leg into the red water.

Madu stops her, "Nipa."

She comes out and stands by the riverbank. She flaps her hair and folds her arms. Madu comes to her, he picks up some cowry beads that had fallen off her hair, and fixes the beads on the loose braids.

"Nipa, why did you leave in anger, I was coming to you with joy."

"I saw you on the bush path, with that chaste maiden. You looked at her lovingly. You do not look at me that way. Your eyes only fill up with lust whenever you are with me. Do you love her?"

"I do not love her."

"Do you love me?" Madu does not answer and Nipa rotates like a whirlwind.

"Nipa stop, do not go." She did not stop. Madu enters the whirlwind and together, they travel to the depth of the sea. He does not have difficulty breathing under water. The motion of the water does not sway him. Madu stands as if he is on land. He takes her hand. Bubbles precede his speech, "Nipa, I do not only love you. I cannot live without you."

"Do you know where we are?"

He spreads his arms, "In the depth of the sea, where my love will cause the end of my existence on earth. I am willing to die for your love. Nipa, I will dare anything for our love. Does this tell you how much I love you?"

Nipa runs into his arms and hugs him tight. Madu wraps his arms around her waist and thinks of the death that will strike him soon. She lets go of him and smiles. She swims beautifully and Madu smiles.

Nipa waves at a whale. The whale swims towards her. They get on the whale's back and sit facing each other. "I thought what you had for me was just carnal intimacy," says Nipa. "Why did you risk your life to be here?"

"When I saw you gather the whirl, my belly trembled because of the fear that I was never going to see you again. My lips quivered at the disappearing tone of your feet. Coldness sipped into my bones. At that moment, I did not care of being captured as a slave in the sea, I stared death in the face, wholeheartedly." He holds her waist, "Do you love me?"

She caresses his cheeks, "How will you ever think I'll not love you? My fear was you didn't love me."

He realises Nipa has not professed her love for him and he release his grip on her. Nipa notices his withdrawal and look up to his eyes. "Nipa do you love me?"

"I love you, Madu, for the affections I feel for you. I will defy the earth and the water."

Madu gathers her into his arms and twirl her around. The whirlwind takes over them and transports them back to land.

Arm in arm, Nipa and Madu reappear on the riverbank. The water becomes pure. He touches all over his body and is shocked red blood still flows in his veins. Nipa is just as speechless until Madu touches her arm.

"Why, I'm still alive?" Madu says. He feels his heartbeat with both hands.

“Guns and traps to the hunter, hook, and sinker to the fisherman. I have no idea, how you successfully captured me from the depth of the ocean and whisked me away without any struggle from the marine gates, wrought by the octopuses. The octopuses would have strangled you to death. The guards of the sea do not show such leniency. Are you a god? How did you come back whole from the sea?”

“I am no god. My magnificent goddess, you were attracted to my edibles.” Nipa blushes. “My love for you is the greatest hooker. Perhaps, the sea guards couldn’t have dared the fires of my gun.”

She smiles, “Your gun is powerless in the water; there is no fire that the ocean cannot quench. You stringed my heart well, my crown. Your affectionate love is what I wanted to eat off your hook.”

Madu kisses her forehead. He looks above her head and frowns. “Your hair, the cowries are gone.”

Nipa anxiously searches for her beads on the hair but none is in place. “How did that happen? My beads are gone.”

“Nipa, your face, your face is shrinking.”

Nipa touches her face; she could not feel the wrinkles that are all over her face. She goes to the clear stream and glares upon her reflection. She beholds her flawless skin and beautiful face. “Madu, you jest, I am me, my beauty is ageless. Madu, take me home before the wind leaves patches all over my body.”

Madu does not want to trouble her mind; Nipa has aged more than his great-grand mother had, before she had passed away. He takes her hand and leads the way to his house. Madu comes through the backyard. Erivwa sees him ushering Nipa into the house. He nods and grins.

"Madu, you brought me home." Nipa twirls around and stops in front of him. She holds his hands and touches each to her cheeks. "Thank you for bringing me closer to your heart, this is a great landmark we have come." She goes into his arms and Madu hugs her warmly.

Her face has grown very thick scales and they are so rough on his smooth cheek. Nipa has aged anciently and the scales look like a crocodile's skin. Nipa begins to play with Madu's nipples; he indulges her, but finds the touch rather repulsive. He is angry with himself. He loves her heart and not her physical appearance.

"Nipa," He gently drops her hands by her sides and caresses them. "You should get some rest. I won't give you water to bath because we have just been vomited from the temple of its source."

Nipa grins, "But Madu, if I don't have a warm bath, I will feel cold. I feel so cold." She wraps her arms around her abdomen.

"I shall set the fire and wrap you in my arms. You would only feel warmth, my love."

"Oh, Madu, I feel great, knowing I'll be spending the night with you, and every other night, right?"

Madu nods. She runs into his arms for another hug and Madu smiles happily. "Nipa, I feel more than happy. Come, and have your rest, it has been a long day."

"Yes, I shall have my rest. But Madu, shall I meet with your parents now, or when the morning hour comes?"

"My father is no longer in this world. You shall meet my family in the morning. You will meet my aunt, cousin and my dearest mother. Erivwa has seen you several times by the stream so he will need fewer introductions." He chuckles.

"Oh, the soft sayings, I am sorry. I hope I've not made you feel uncomfortable about your father."

"Nipa, I will feel all right if you come to bed."

"No, I will help you start the fire." Nipa gets some woods by the door and set the firewood in-between cold stones.

Madu smiles appreciatively and uses the lamp oil to light the hearth. He rubs his palms to drive away cold and carries Nipa into his arms before she thinks of another task to accomplish. Nipa makes no protest as he lays her on the bed made of padded fur. Madu goes to lock the door and comes back to lie beside her. He lovingly caresses her face and thinks on what to do about the rapid agedness breaking her face. He hugs her and concludes on going to the cave to see the sorcerer.

Chapter Twenty-Eight

Before dawn, Madu wakes. It is the same beautiful Nipa he sees lying next to him. But she is in her naked form, and her braids have come completely loose. He brushes her hair with his fingers to untangle the locks.

The water goddesses had been angry at Nipa's decision to fall in love with a mortal, more so, their dismay when Madu entered the depth of the realm and returned to land alive. All the anger and arguments they had, had been breaking Nipa's face. The goddesses had wrestled to extract their bloodline from her cells. They tried to disown and strip her off all rights but they were not successful. They could only take away her aquatic garb and seashell crowns from her hair.

Madu covers her with a blanket. He is pleased she is back to normal. He adds woods to the dying embers and fans it until it flared afire. Madu sets his hunting tools. He does not have a reason to get up early and go to the cave. Nipa is well. He gets back on the bed and falls into a peaceful sleep.

In the sea, water drums beat so fast while a calabash containing water falls off Madu's table and crashes on the floor. Nipa and Madu toss in bed until daybreak.

Nipa is the first to wake. She rolls over and cuddles Madu. He stirs and she caresses his cheeks with hers. “All night, I battled with the goddesses of the sea. None of them wanted our relationship to be, but my mother was of great support. She accepts you, Madu. She asked me to go back to where my heart can beat beautifully. My mother is one adamant and conventional ruler, I thought she would have been the first to condemn my actions and disown me, but she prodded me to go on. She is pleading to the goddesses that they accept our relationship.”

“I’m not surprised, that is the heart of a mother. I wish they would accept our union wholeheartedly. Get up, Nipa. Freshen up. I will introduce you to my family, soon.”

“Great, I cannot wait to meet them.” She excitedly gets off the bed. “Where do you have your toilet?”

“In here,” he opens a door that leads to a small room that has a chamber pot and pots of water. There is a narrow hole on the floor and a small opening for ventilation. Nipa smiles at him and goes in.

Madu meets his mother in her garden. She is harvesting some vegetables-tomatoes and pepper. He takes the basket from her and holds it. Umota drops tomatoes into the basket and dusts her hands.

She smiles at him. “Madu, how are you?”

“I am great, Mother.”

She holds his chin and peers into his eyes, “but you look like a child that did not have sufficient sleep. Did Erivwa keep you up at night?”

“Mother, Erivwa does not sleep in my hut. He goes to his mother after I tell him stories about wars and great fishermen."

She nods, "You rarely step into my garden. I hope all is well?"

"Yes, mother. I want you to meet someone."

"Have you found the girl that would give me grandchildren and give you great companionship for life?"

"Mother, you are always hasty."

"Have I not been patient enough? Erivwa has given me the joy of grand-motherhood. He is growing into a man." She grimaces, "these days, he does not allow me bath him. So I need babies I can bath and carry on my back." She smiles, "tell me, Madu. Does she have good qualities of a wife and daughter-in-law? She has to be the best for us."

"If you do not come with me, how will you find out?" Madu puts the basket on his shoulder and they leave.

Oma and Nipa are already chatting. Erivwa is grinning at their discussion.

"And when the rabbit roared, the lion ran and hid behind the rat," Nipa says.

"Wow that is impossible. Nipa, that is so not possible," Erivwa laughs and waves his hands in disagreement.

"Nipa, meet my mother."

Nipa stands and folds her arms, "greetings to you, mother."

Umota appraises her and nods satisfactorily, "she is so beautiful.

Madu, I have not seen this face around the village."

"Mother, she is not from this land."

"I thought as much. Madu, have you offered her some water to drink and food to eat? She is here early. I bet she did not wait to have breakfast at her house before coming to see you."

"Grandma, there is no need for that. Nipa slept in brother Madu's hut. He must have fed her with enough fishes and meat." Nipa and Madu blushes.

"What, she did not come from her house?" Umota looks from Madu to Nipa.

Oma clears her throat. Umota suspiciously glances at Oma. Oma shakes her head.

"Erivwa, take that basket from your uncle and bring it to the kitchen."

"Okay, grandma. Do you want to prepare soup? I am very hungry for your soup."

"Yes, my lovely boy. I am making soup for you." She ruffles Erivwa's hair.

Madu gives Erivwa the basket and he runs off to the kitchen.

"Nipa, make yourself more comfortable," says Umota.

"No, I will come with you," says Nipa.

"Okay, I will be in my hut." Madu bobs and leaves.

Nipa follows Oma and Umota to the kitchen. They slice the vegetables while chatting. Erivwa arranges the stove. He breathes out and fire comes out from his mouth. The women are shocked.

"Erivwa, what did you just do?" Oma asks.

"Mother, I saw fire come out of my mouth. Did I ignite the fire?" He points at the burning stove.

"This is amazing, Erivwa, you have supernatural powers," Nipa says excitedly.

"Wow, oh, that's cool." Erivwa inhales deeply…

"No, Erivwa stop..." Erivwa blows out with great force and fire roars out of his mouth. He collapses. "Erivwa," Oma shouts and runs to his side. "Erivwa, wake up, wake up," she slaps his cheeks.

Umota sprinkles water on his face. Nipa runs off to call Madu.

Erivwa's body is on fire. He can feel someone rubbing his face with wet cloth. He unsuccessfully lifts a hand to stop the process. He makes an effort to open his eyes but the wet cloth touches his eyes. Every part of his body screams of pain as he tries to remember where he is and what has happened to him.

He moves slowly, his limbs are going through torrents of agony. Erivwa stops moving and lay still. Madu sees Erivwa's situation and goes to call an herbal doctor.

"This is beyond herbs and ointment. He does not suffer from any ailment." The herbal doctor asks, "Who is his mother?"

Oma comes forward, "I am his mother."

The herbal doctor closes her eyes, "Who is his father?"

"Erin, Erin is his father."

She opens her eyes, "Hmmm, he is part human and half god. I would not be able to do anything. The fate of the boy's recovery is beyond me. You should seek Demimo."

Erivwa remains unconscious for three days. Umota invites the priest to discern the fate of Erivwa. Demimo throws some cowries on the floor and put the cowries against one another. He gives up and packs all the charms into a bag.

"I have tried to reweave his destiny but many forces are at odds to see him doomed." He enters a trance. "They have refused to grant me access. They alter my charms to dis-enable me from travelling with his spirit." With his eyes unmoving, Demimo opens the bag and brings out a white yarn. He speedily weaves a fine tapestry but the thread keeps loosening, "this is bigger than my prowess." He fearfully opens his eyes and Erivwa gasps and immediately enters into the world of spirits.

All around him are scribbles on ancient stones. The room glitters. He sees the burning furnace. The fire sparks and roars. The heat in the room increases.

Erivwa looks down at his sweaty body. He goes further into the room. There is a wooden box near the furnace. He touches the locket on his chest and places a hand on the box. He chants some scriptures. Green arrays of light emanates from the box.

"Erivwa, this is the soul of your father. The god of vengeance and thunderbolt," there is thunderclap, "I am the god of vengeance trapped in this furnace," there is a savage roar.

"You are not what you think you are. Your weakness is born from your mortality. Your strength is immortal. You are indestructible; you are a power of the sun, and cloud. Heaven and earth are full of your existence." A scroll rises from the box and hangs mid-air. "I will make you see what others cannot see. Possess your principality and powers. Take back your strength."

Erivwa opens his mouth and dose of fire goes down his throat. He spreads his fingers and bolts of thunder clings to his nails. His eyes shine like the fire in the furnace. Some ancestors' apparition appears. Their palms gather all the heat in the room. They stone the heat into Erivwa's heart.

Erivwa shivers as a great source of energy overwhelms him. He screams and raises his eyes to the roof. The shrine dissolves into a green field. Erivwa falls to the ground. All the powers absorb into his body. He is conscious of the surrounding for a while. A cutlass drops in-between his feet. He raises his head wearily and studies the blunt cutlass. He faints.

"Now, I know what it is. Madu must go to Igowe and free the roaring fire in the furnace," says Demimo, "and he must go with the offspring of the fire that roars recurrently in Igowe." Oma gasps. He nods at her. Oma quickly grasps Erivwa to her bosom.

Chapter Twenty-Nine

Days go by. Erivwa's eyes become red. When anyone offends him, he flies into rage. His temper is as fiery as his red eyes; no one except his mother can look him straight in his eyes, his father's totem dances in his eyeballs.

Erivwa becomes very strong and more handsome; his slightest anger causes furious thunderbolts, and injures any unfortunate person it meets on the way. His temper makes people stay away and disassociates from any activities he is involved. He strikes out before thinking, and his bolts strikes directly into a person's heart.

Madu comes to Oma, "Oma, I think we should let Erivwa go to Igowe. You had heard what Demimo said, right?"

"I heard him."

"Erivwa will go to Igowe."

Oma cries, "No he will not. I do not want to lose my son. If he goes to Igowe, I will lose him."

"Staying in Gwons, leaving for Igowe; either ways, you will lose him. Oma, have you seen Erivwa of late? His uncontrollable power will kill him or the people of Gwons will try every way possible to eliminate him. I am leaving for Igowe. I will take Erivwa with me."

Nipa appears. "I shall come with you."

Madu nods at her and smiles, "we will leave before dawn."

Madu goes away. Nipa kneels before Oma and consoles her.

Madu talks to Erivwa and he agrees to come with him to Igowe. "Erivwa, I know you are haunted. Just as I have a nightmare bugging me. I am glad you will go to Igowe. I am so proud of you, you grew stronger than I imagined." Erivwa smiles weakly. Madu hugs him tight.

Oma packs her bag. She has decided to go with her son. She meets them outside. Erivwa smiles and hugs his mother. Madu and Nipa nod. Umota cries and waves them off. Demimo joins them at the exit of Gwons.

"I want to accompany Erivwa to Igowe. At first, to divine his fate was bigger than I was until we broke through. I want to be present, in case he needs my help to scale through," says Demimo.

"Thank you, wise one. Your presence has eased my mind a little," says Oma.

Erivwa reassuringly squeezes his mother's hands.

Chapter Thirty

They journey to Igowe on rented horses. They reach the kingdom by midday. The horses slow down on the rocks. Erivwa's eyes sparkles at the resplendent mountains and rocks.

"Oma, where can we find the source of our mission?" asks Demimo.

Oma sighs and silently leads them to the Shrine of Igowe. The fire roars.

They enter the shrine. The fire seems to sparkle excitedly in green and blue flames. Erivwa leaves everyone behind and walks towards the furnace. The fire roars, Oma begins to cry.

"I knew that you will come here," Keme appears. "I have waited so long." His hair has become dreadlocks. He is in shabby clothing.

"Keme, you are here?"

"Oma, always bleating my name, Meee…Meee…" he says insanely and draws a sword.

"Keme, what are you doing?" Oma asks.

Keme screams and charges at Oma, "I was not successful in killing Erin, I have waited all these years hoping to kill him but it would please me to kill you instead."

Erivwa quickly takes Madu's dagger, runs, and steps in his mother's front. Keme runs into the dagger and gasps. The fire roars. Keme shouts and four octopus limbs stick out of his mouth to grab Erivwa. It twists Erivwa's neck and his eyes become bloodshot.

Nipa's legs transforms into a very long fishtail and battles with the octopus limbs. The octopus lets go of Erivwa. The octopus limbs quickly grab Oma and fling her into the burning furnace. "Mother," Erivwa screams in shock. He shivers at Oma's cries.

The fire roars angrily and rises. The roof opens, and two dragons burst out of the furnace. The dragons have the faces of Erin and Oma. They roar out fire through their nostrils and fly out of the shrine.

Erivwa is the first to run outside, the others soon follow him. The dragons hang mid-air and flap their heavy wings. Tears gather in Oma's eyes. As the tears are about to slip, Erin catches the tear drops with his wing. Erin roars, and they fly into the cloud.

"There shall be a great battle in the upper world. Erin has gone to take over his throne," says Demimo. "Madu, you are now the boy's father."

Keme runs out of the shrine, Erivwa angrily turns around and releases tons of thunderbolts into Keme's heart. Keme slumps and dies. His body turns into a crow and disappears. Nipa and Madu flank Erivwa. Demimo stands behind them.

www.ingramcontent.com/pod-product-compliance
Lightning Source LLC
Chambersburg PA
CBHW032001170626
46807CB00006B/2587
* 9 7 8 9 7 8 5 6 0 9 5 4 7 *